Dalogrenant

inscribed and illuminated by

Gillian Cameron

Book the Second: Maiden Britannia

SDP
STACKED DECK PRESS

Published by Stacked Deck Press
SDP00005

ISBN 978-0-9970487-5-9

It says something about a person that she would choose to communicate her highest hopes and deepest dreams through art.

How curious, also, that the craft in which she dabbles as a storyteller is a clever cartoon, an anachronistic transgender medieval mashup. And how fabulous that the character driving this beautifully composed and sharp-witted online comic strip is, like its creator, wise, wily and a woman with an unorthodox origin.

A school teacher by trade, a lover of long ago history and antiquity as well as art, Gillian Cameron is like me, a Southern California transplant and a parent. Even before retiring from public education, she harnessed her passions into rocket fuel for a second career, her first as a transgender woman.

I have had the honor of knowing Gillian far more than a fortnight, which even I know means two weeks (right, Siri?). We first met, as most trans people do, on the social media platform of Facebook, adding our witty competing comments on the posts of mutual friends, and connected in the autumn of 2014.

My reputation was at that time in tatters, having gone from being the first trans journalist in TV network news to transition in public, to the first one to get fired. But instead of riding the bandwagon of people who enjoy seeing people trip, fall—and fall hard—Gillian extended her hand in virtual friendship, and not nine months later did so again in person, even offering a weary coast to coast traveler a couch on which to crash.

This is an angel, you see, whose hand divines the derring-do of a fantastic Arthurian world, where being transgender is not the arc of each story, but just one critical part of this central character of Calogrenant—Cally, if you please. Gillian has faithfully recast a round table of allies and enemies and set them on adventures that prominently feature her transformed knight, who seeks understanding, acceptance and validation of her identity as a maiden; it is, she once wrote, the fulfillment of a secret desire.

Being transgender to me is as significant now as the color of my eyes, my ethnic heritage, and the kind of car I drive. It is but one aspect of who I am and does not define me. This is a character trait I find in my closest friends, of which Gillian ranks highest of all, and for this I am a very fortunate maiden. Transgender isn't what Gillian is, nor does it define either the artist nor her creation. I'd say you're more apt to find more comedy in this comic than gender dysphoria, although gender stereotypes are a frequent foil, and justifiably so.

But what I love most about the character of Cally is how steeped she is in authentic Arthurian tradition and the magical tales that her creator loves most in all the world. If not for having to lose computer-aided technology and online interaction, not to mention modern clothing choices, I'd say Gillian would be most equipped of all those I know to survive time travel to this 13th century world.

The universe of *Calogrenant* has many ties to our world, by design: Cally is referred to enemies by as "it," she endures mansplaining in almost every panel and she is determined to break the stain glass castle ceiling that keeps her from being both maiden and knight of the table round.

My heart leapt early on in the series, when the newly minted maiden found books from the future in her boudoir, one of which cast a spell on me early in my transition: the landmark transgender memoir *She's Not There* by my mentor and friend Jennifer Finney Boylan. Ever since, it has been my eternal wish that Cally might someday herself be transported to our world, ever briefly, for an adventure that might even bring her face to face with her creator.

I wish for this because of all the amazing characters in my wonderful life, none could be more exciting for the maiden to meet than my friend, Gillian Cameron.

I hope you enjoy the merry ride in the pages that follow!

Dawn Ennis
West Hartford, Connecticut, November 2016

Dawn Ennis is an award-winning journalist and is currently Assistant Editor at LGBTQ Nation, *Writer/Producer at* advocate.com, *and a Writer for* NBCOUT, BuzzFeed, *and* NewNowNext. *Her own thoughts can be read at* lifeafterdawn.com.

Incipit Liber Secundus

For Michelle Franklin Davis, a steadfast ally and a dear friend who I never got to know as well as I'd liked or as she deserved.

JRR Tolkien said of *The Lord of the Rings* that the "tale grew in the telling." Though I would never dream of comparing myself with that scholar and master storyteller, I can say that Calogrenant's story has done the same thing. Relating Cally's tale and living vicariously through her is as much an adventure for me as it is for her. Like Cally, I had only the vaguest idea of what lay in store for her upon leaving Camelot or what exactly she would lean under the tutelage of Morgan le Fay. Of Morgan herself, I had only a vague outline, based upon her shadowy portrayals in the medieval romances, and a question that has bothered me since my teen years: If she is such an enemy of King Arthur, why is she on the barge with the other queens, bearing him to Avalon? Telling a story, for me, is about descovery; the characters come alive for me, and I follow them, watch what they do, and listen to what they say. Very often, I am pleased to say, I am surprised. So this is the second book of Cally's adventures, and I hope you have as much fun with it as I have.

Great thanks to...

Dawn Ennis, my dear friend whose foreword graces this volume; Tara Avery of Stacked Deck Press, who can gently light fires undeer me; Ted Abenheim and the wonderful folks at Prism Comics; Professor Helen Nicholson, mentor, supporter, source and friend; Samantha Quinn, a bastion of support as always; Melody Friend, the real Mistress Puissance; True Thomas the Storyteller (aka Rob Seutter) talespinner and resource; Hank Mayo, Darlie Brewster, Jayna L-Ponder, Dana Marie Andra, Emily Michels, John Ellis, Jim Bradbury, Sparky Santos, Paul McGhee, Christianne Benedict, and William Feisterman, who constantly inspire me to improve my craft; Allison Vought, mother confessor and Photoshop mentor; Jennell Jaquays and Rebecca Heineman for their expertise and insight: Jayne De Menthe, Karen Tate, Karen Estremo, Denise Dumars, Joan de Artemis, Lori Cadena, Kat Robb, Aniitra Ravenmoon, Aostara Kay, Jennifer Graf, Shelli H. English, Lauren Alvarado, and Billie Sage – as fine a group of magical ladies as one could hope to find dancing in the woods by the light of the moon - their magic inspires me; dear colleagues and friends who have given me invaluable support and commentary: Jeff Davis, Lee Patterson, Rachel Regalado, Alyssa Guthrie, Sarah Schnorr, Lana Moore, Abigail Jensen, Rhada Smith, Lynne Hurd Bryant, Paula Warner, Lisa Euphrates, Dugan Manor, Rachel Heyburn, Jenifer Divine, Darya Teasewell, Michelle Trout, John Breen, Zoe Ellen Brain, Kay Garcia, Peter Weeks, Gail Catherine MacNiell, Joanne Lara, Coline Russell, Rachel So, Zoe Parker, Philip Haxo, Jimmy Lindberg, Paula Randol-Smith, Maria-Katriina Lehtinen, Betty Ott, Penny Wilhelm, Paula Gannon, Adana Gardner, Barry Shils, Doran George, and so many more; and, of course, Karen, Rachel, Emily, Steven, and Conor.

Thank you everyone for your support and love!

Gillian Cameron

Here beginneth Book II
ye King's Head
MY LADY I WOULD HAVE THEE TAKE CARE. THERE BE MANY BRIGANDS TWIXT HERE AND GORRE.
GOOD HOST, I THANK THEE FOR THY HOSPITALTY AND THY CARE. FEAR NOT FOR ME, I PRAY THEE. I KNOW THE WAY WELL.

POOR LASS... ALONE ON THE ROAD WITH ALL THAT GOLD... AH, BUT SHE CAN NEVER SAY SHE WENT WITHOUT WARNIN', EH?

ye King's Head

CLASH!
CLANG!
PARRY
THRUST
CRUNCH!
(OW!)

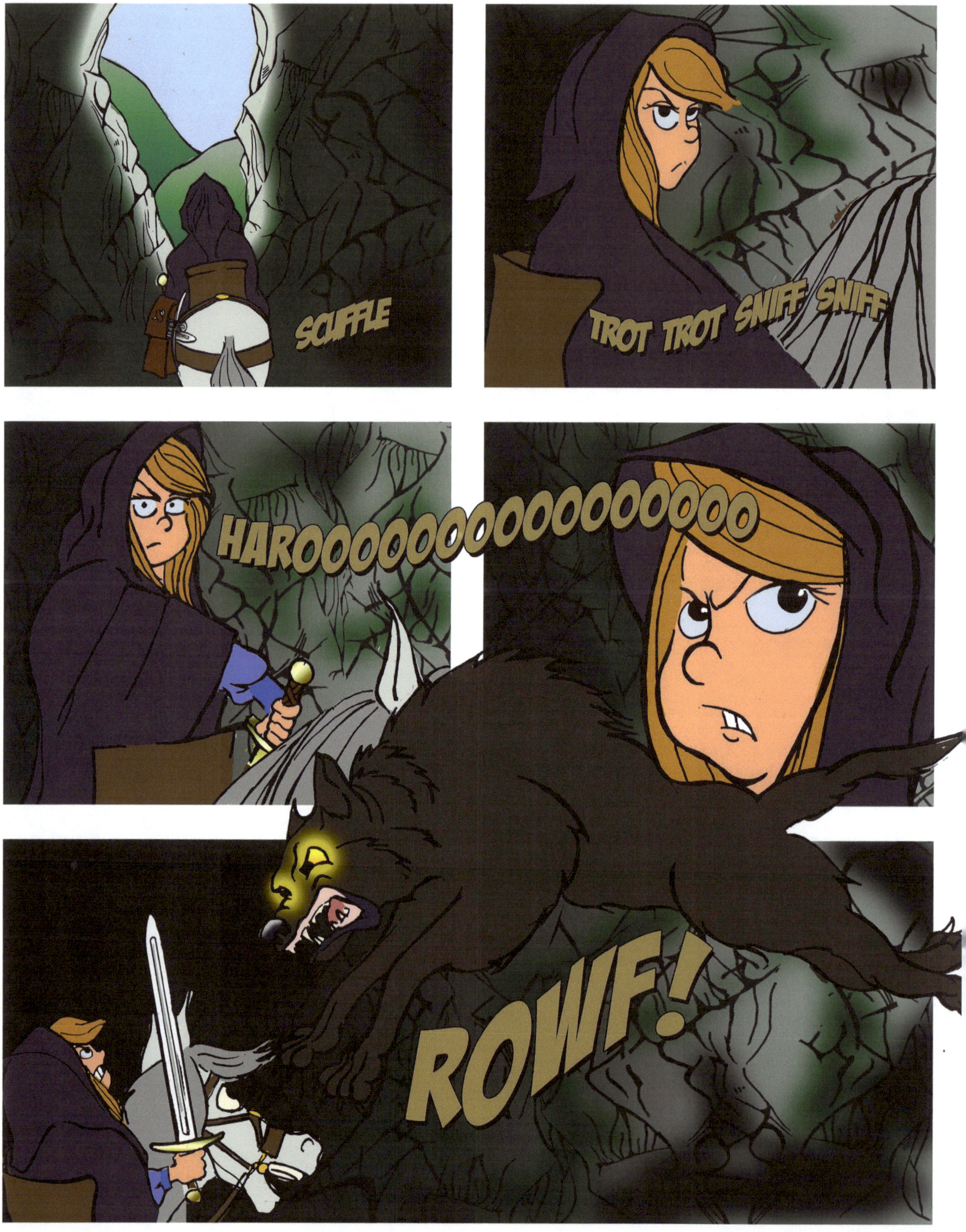

HAROOOOOOOOOOOOOOOO

ROWF!

WHOOSH!

mnf?
WHUMP!

SPLERP

PHUTT

FWUMP

OH, INDEED?

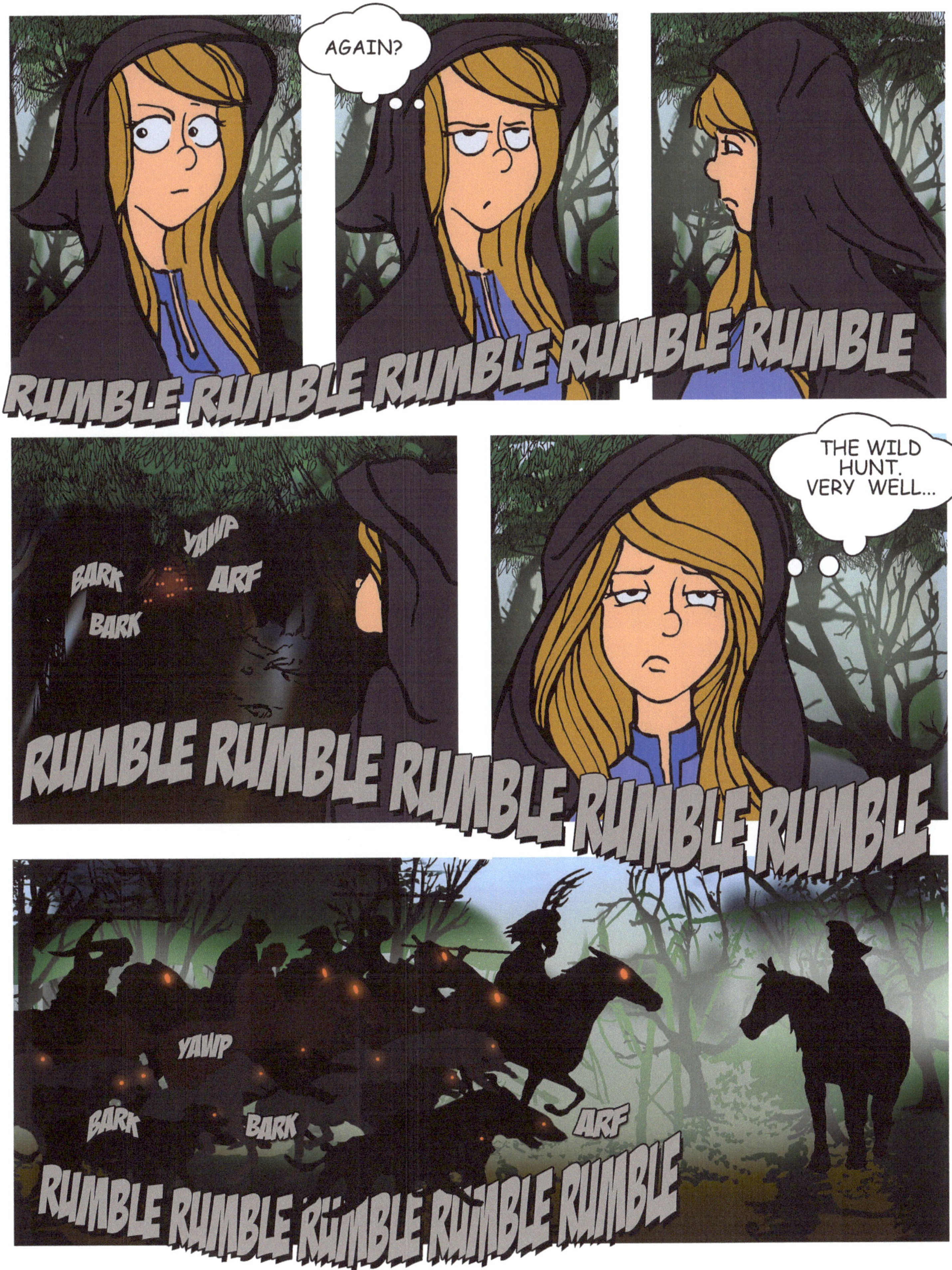

YAWP
BARK
ARF
BARK
THE WILD HUNT. VERY WELL...
RUMBLE RUMBLE RUMBLE RUMBLE RUMBLE

YAWP
BARK
BARK
ARF
RUMBLE RUMBLE RUMBLE RUMBLE RUMBLE

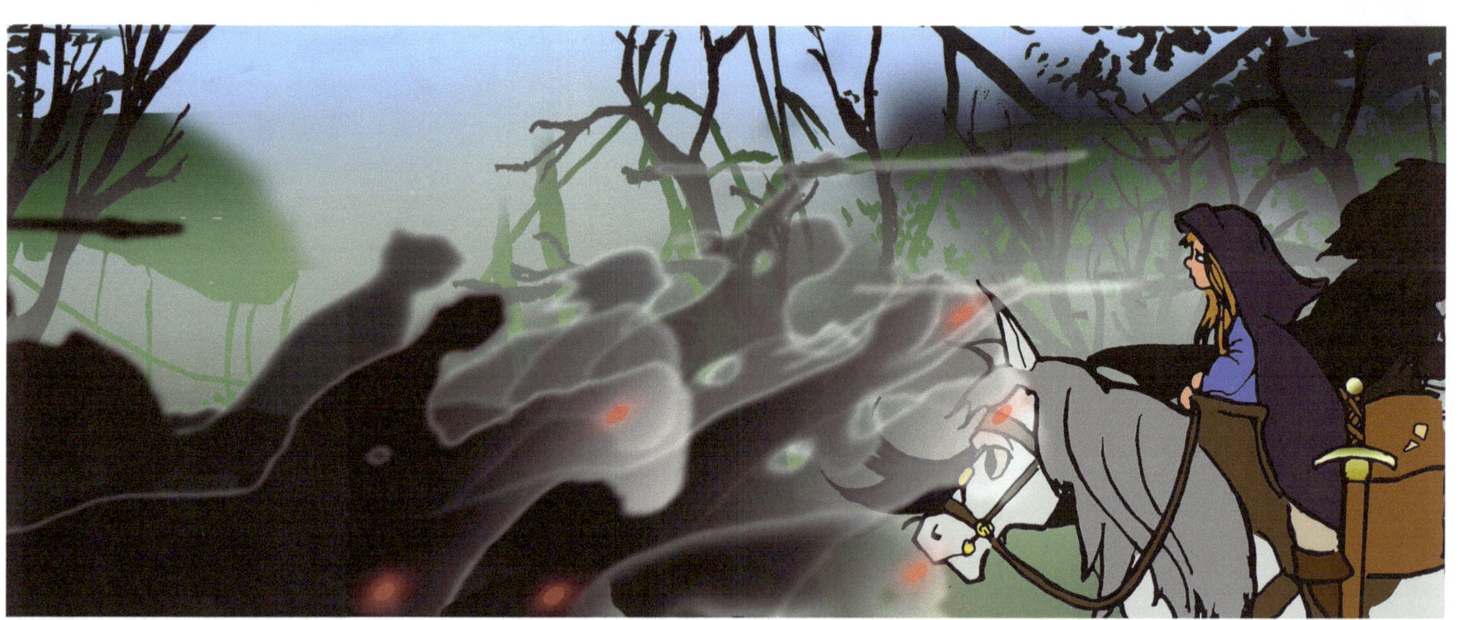

SNAP

A WORD, I PRAY THEE, GOOD MY LORD.

METHINKS, MY LORD, IF THOU WOULDST HAVE ME DEAD, I SHOULD NEVER HAVE LEFT BROCELIANDE ALIVE. NAY, EVEN IF THOU SHOULDST HAVE ME HARMED, THOU WOULDST NOT BESET ME WITH GLAMOURS AND FOOLS. MY LADY OF BROCELIANDE SPAKE TO ME OF THY VOW UNTO HER. I SUSPECT THOU DOTH SPORT WITH ME, AND I FEAR NO HARM AT THY HANDS

I KNOW OF THINE IRE, BUT IN BEING WHO I AM, I MEAN NO SLIGHT TO THEE. AS THOU DOST HONOR THY WORD TO MY LADY, SO I PLEDGE THEE MINE HONOR AND GIVE GREAT THANKS FOR MY SAFE CONDUCT.

A BOW OF FAIRY MAKE! A FINE GIFT AND UNLOOKED FOR!
SAXON RAIDERS? PICTS? BRIGANDS? GALLOWGLASSES? KERNS?
TARGET PRACTICE!
SHHHTHP! SHHHTHP! SHHHTHP! SHHHTHP! SHHHTHP! SHHHTHP! SHHHTHP!
THE ARROWS DO REPLENISH THEMSELVES IN THE SHEAF. I LIKE THIS WELL.

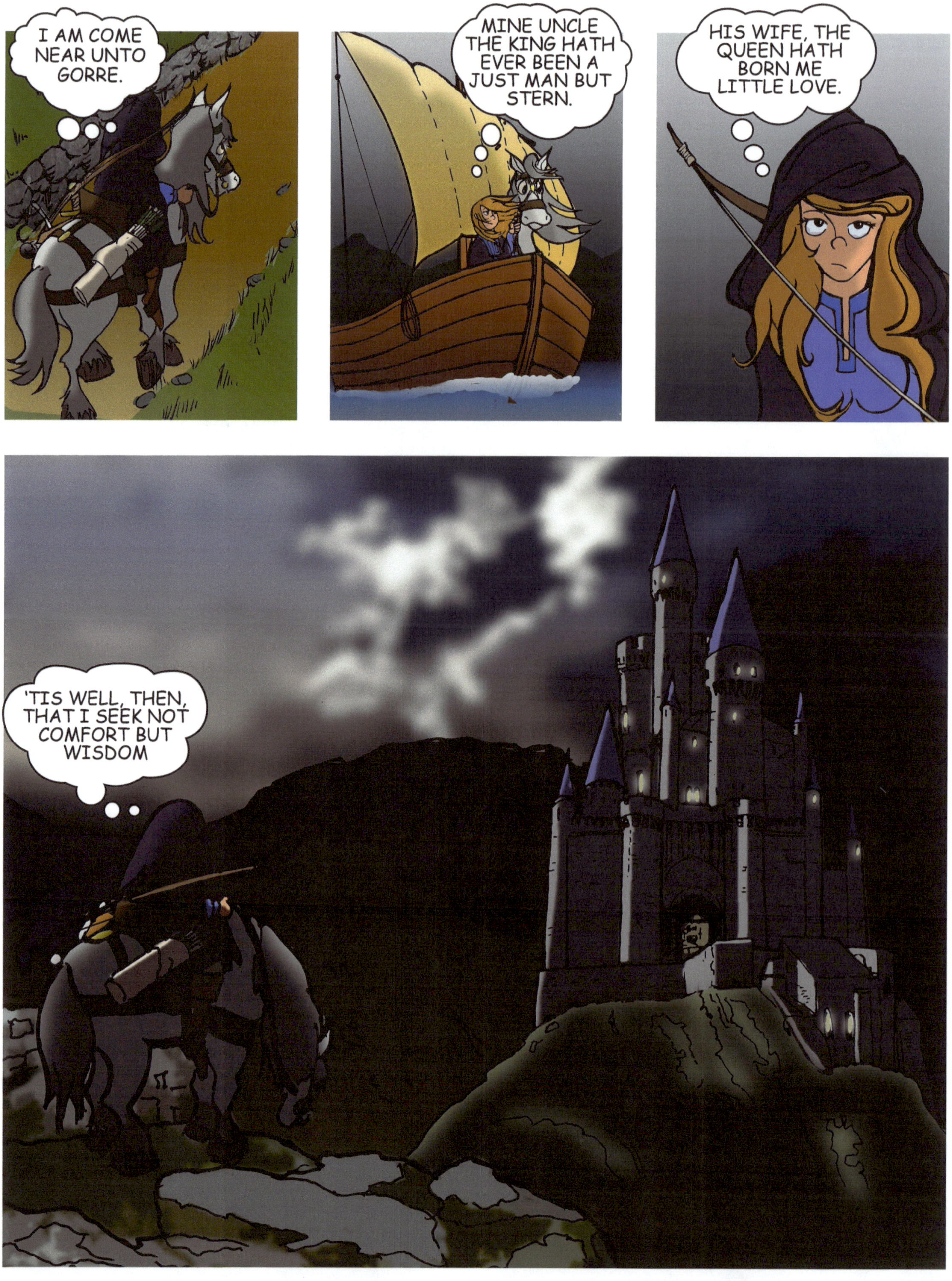

'TIS WELL, THEN, THAT I SEEK NOT COMFORT BUT WISDOM

UNCLE?

MY LORD OF GORRE, WHAT HATH WROUGHT THIS CHANGE IN THEE?

LA BELLE DAME SANS MERCI HATH HIM IN THRALL.

ACCOLON! DOST THOU MOCK THY LIEGE AND HIS LADY?

GOOD CALOGRENANT, THOUGH JEST I MAY, I DO NOT MOCK. I SPEAK TRUE. THINE UNCLE, KING URIENS, HATH A GLAMOUR UPON HIM, AND THE QUEEN HATH A THRALL IN ME AS WELL. SHE HERSELF WILL TELL THEE NO LESS.

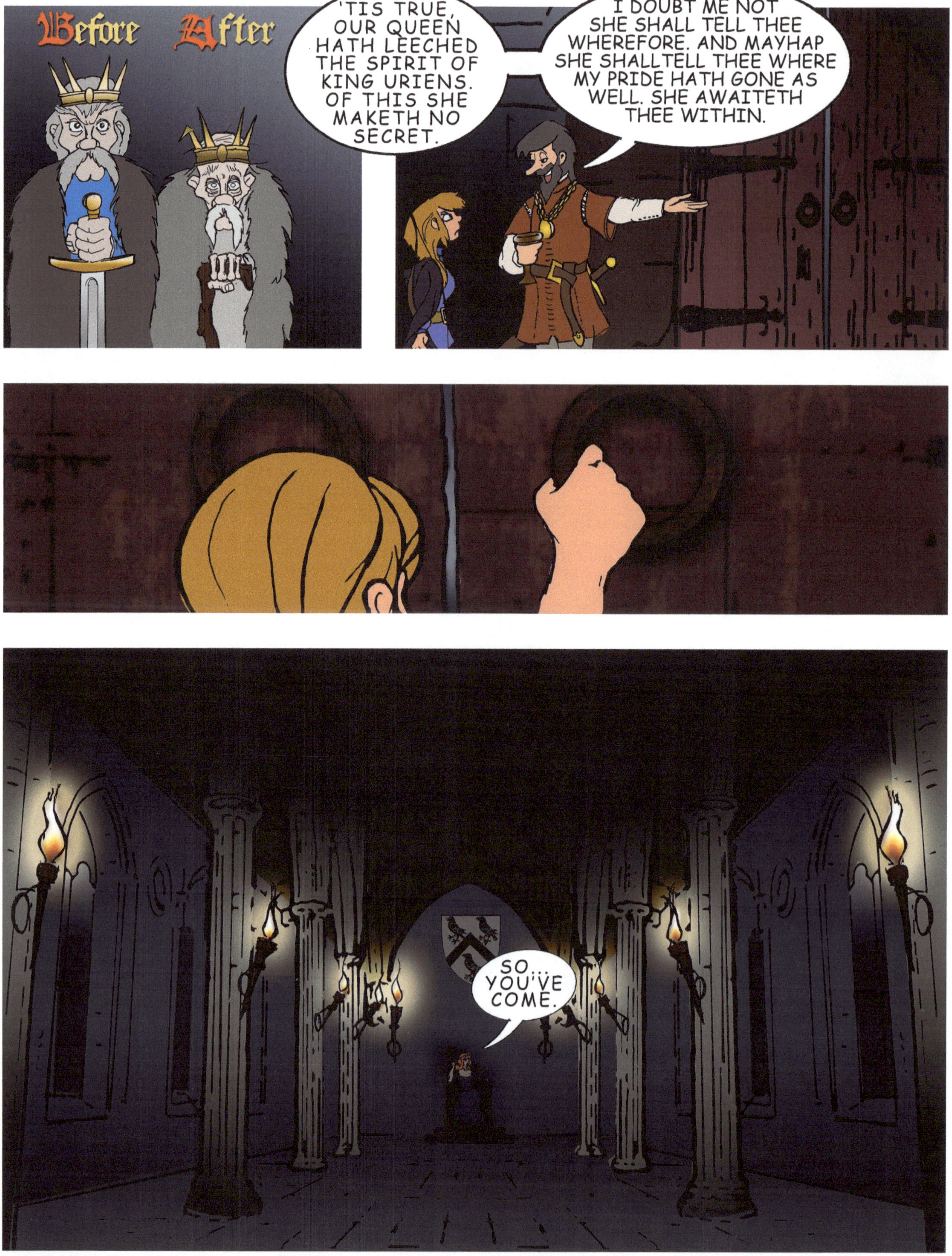

SO... YOU'VE COME.

"SIR" CALOGRENANT! YOU HAVE CHANGED PROFOUNDLY SINCE LAST I SAW YOU.
AYE, MY QUEEN. SO I HAVE.
...AND THOU, QUEEN MORGAN LE FAY, HAST NOT CHANGED ONE WHIT IN ALL MY MEMORY..

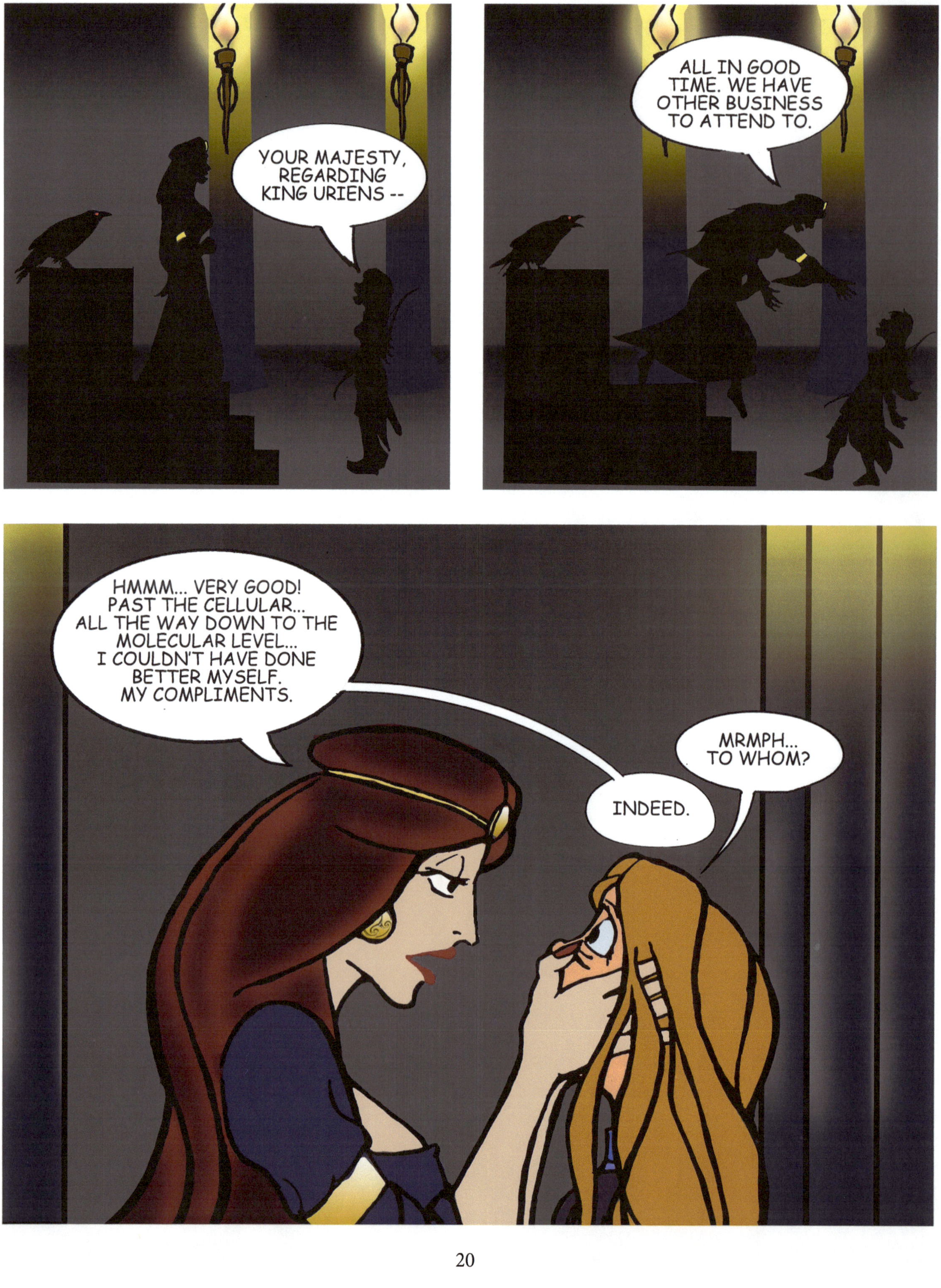

HMMM... VERY GOOD! PAST THE CELLULAR... ALL THE WAY DOWN TO THE MOLECULAR LEVEL... I COULDN'T HAVE DONE BETTER MYSELF. MY COMPLIMENTS.

MRMPH... TO WHOM?

INDEED.

I AM FLATTERED "SIR KNIGHT," THAT YOU COME TO ME FOR TUTELAGE.

MY QUEEN, I COME AT SIR ACCOLON'S BIDDING AND LORD MYRDDYN'S DIRECTION, BUT HAVING SEEN MINE UNCLE THE KING, I WONDER AT THE WISDOM OF THIS JOURNEY

You dare to -

AYE. STRIKE ME, MY QUEEN. I AM SURE SIR ACCOLON TOLD YOU OF HIS EXPERIENCE WITH ME. LET US SEE WHAT OCCURS.

CENSORED

SO MUCH FOR NICETIES. COME. WE'VE MUCH WORK. FOLLOW -- AND DO ME THE THE KINDNESS OF NOT MENTIONING YOUR DAMNABLE UNCLE AGAIN, IF NOT INDEFINATELY, AT LEAST FOR TWO TURNS OF THE HOURGLASS.

YES, "SIR" CALOGRENANT, SIR ACCOLON HAS REPORTED TO ME OF YOUR POWERS. WE SHALL TEST THAT. YOU SHALL LEARN OTHER THINGS AS WELL...

YOUR MAJESTY, I PRAY THEE, DO NOT MOCK ME SO. KING ARTHUR WOULD NOT HAVE A WOMAN AT HIS TABLE. THUS HAVE I LOST MY KNIGHTHOOD. YET EVEN SO, I HAVE MY VOWS RESWORN. CHANGED THOUGH I AM, I YET HAVE THE HEART OF A KNIGHT. I WILL SERVE MY KING, AND I FEAR NOTHING.

I COULD WEEP. IF THE LOSS PAINS YOU SO STRONGLY, I COULD EASILY TRANSFORM YOU BACK TO A MALE.

You wouldn't. Would you?

AND THUS IS THE PECKING ORDER ASSERTED. COME, "MY LADY." LET'S TO WORK.

MY BOUDOIR,
IF YOU WILL..

AND WHAT, AGAIN, IS THE SUBJECT OF THIS TUTELAGE?
LORD MYRDDYN DID SAY WOMEN'S WISDOM AND MORE.

I MAY HAVE A WORD OR TWO WITH LORD MYRDDYN REGARDING CURRICULUM AND WHO DICTATES IT.

SO... MY LADY, YOU ARE HAPPY TO BE A WOMAN, THEN?
IN FAITH, YOUR MAJESTY, 'TIS THE FULFILLMENT OF MY MOST ARDENT WISH!

YOU ARE AN IDIOT!

BUT I SUPPOSE EVEN SUCH AS YOU MAY BE TAUGHT. PUT YOUR WEAPONS BY AND FOLLOW.
THE WATERS OF THIS FONT EMANATE FROM DEEP INSIDE THE MOTHER, AND HER WISDOM MAY BE READ THEREIN.
CLEAR YOUR MIND, AND GAZE INTO THE DEPTHS. GIVE UP ALL YOUR WILL AND SEND YOUR MIND AND SOUL INTO THE WATERS.
AND THE FIRST BIT OF "WOMEN'S WISDOM" I CAN IMPART TO YOU IS THIS:
EXPECT BETRAYAL!

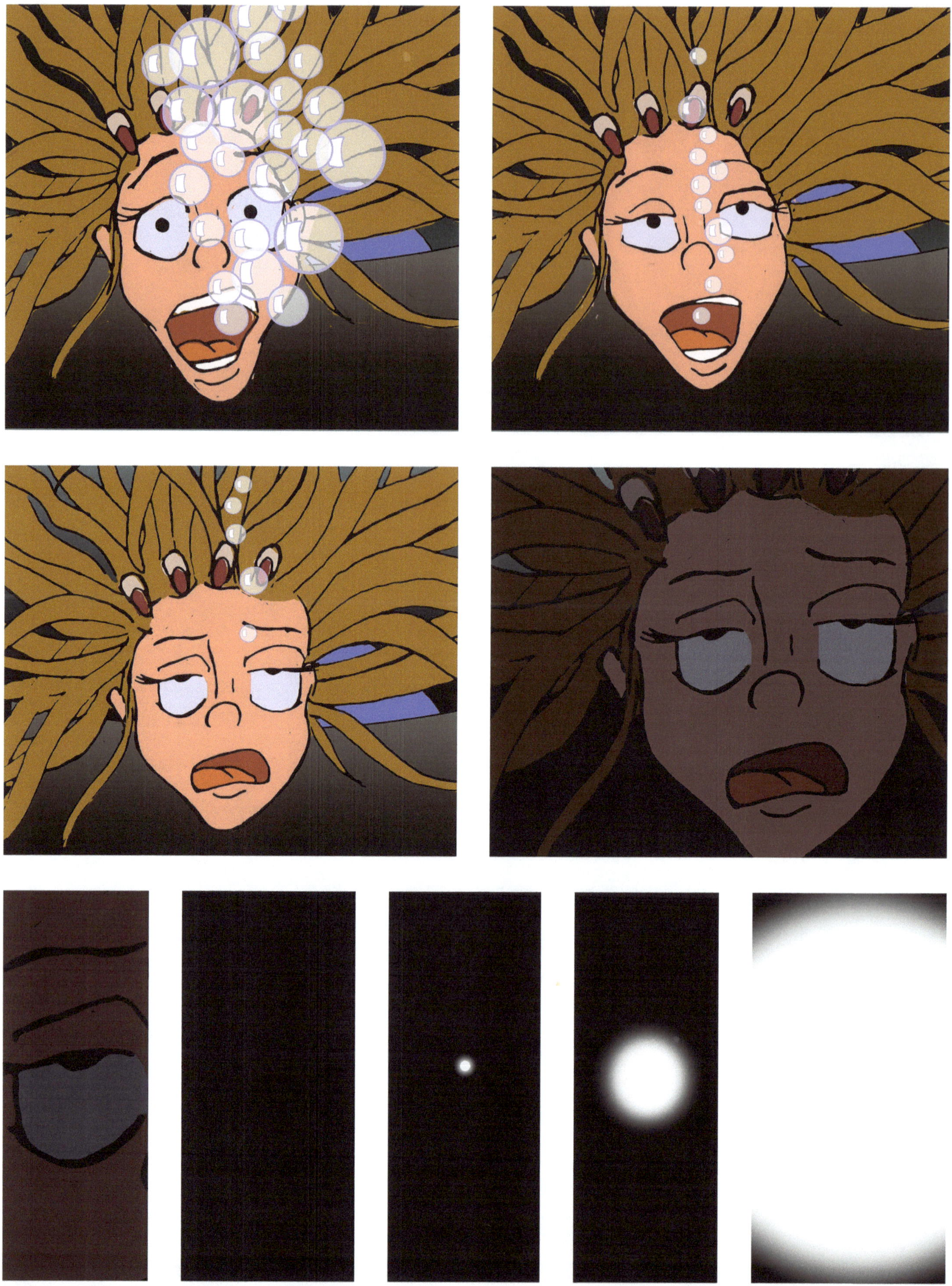

PANT! PANT!
AIEEEEEEEE!
CALM AND STEADY, BELOVED LADY. THY SON IS NEARLY HERE.
BEHOLD! HIS HEAD! AND... OHH!
(THE SEER SAID 'TWAS TO BE A MANCHILD.)
(THE SEER SAID WRONG. THE GREAT ONE WILL BE WRATHFUL.)
(IS THERE NO OTHER WAY?)
(THOU KNOWEST THERE IS NOT. IT IS HER LIFE OR ALL OF OURS.)
WHEREFORE DOST THOU WHISPER? WHAT IS AMISS?
WAAAAAAAAAAAAAAAAAAAAAAAAAAAH!
MY LADY, IT MUST BE DONE.
FORGIVE US, LITTLE ONE.
NO!
WAAAAA-MMMPHH!

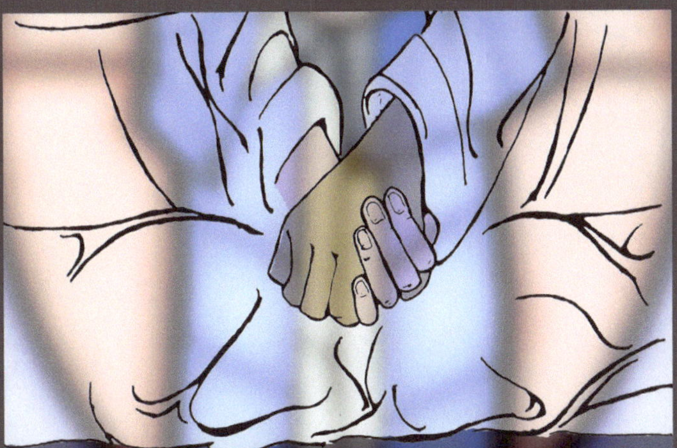

HE HAS BEEN DEALT WITH. BUT IT WAS YOUR LUST -
BROTHER, HE TOOK ME AND -

MY LUST! MOTHER AND THE WOMEN CUT OUT MY LUST WHEN I WAS A CHILD

BROTHER, HOW SHALL I LIVE WITH THE SHAME OF THIS?

YOU SHALL NOT LIVE IN SHAME! AND NEITHER SHALL THE FAMILY!

I AM NOT A MAN, BUT A WOMAN.
WE SHALL PREPARE THE TESTS AND CEREMONIES TO BE CERTAIN, BUT WE ARE TRULY BLESSED IF IT IS SO!
A LHAMANA! A TWO-SPIRIT!

O BELOVED OF THE GODS, PLEASE BLESS OUR WEDDING!

VILE CATAMITE! THOU HAST NO RIGHT TO LIVE!

Gillian
Cameron

SO...
ARE YOU WISE?
GASP

UUNGH!

I HAVE LIVED THE LIVES OF A THOUSAND WOMEN

PAIN, GRIEF, SLAVERY, IGNOMINY. THERE IS NOT A JOY OR A GRACE BUT IT COMETH AT A PRICE.

AND YET YOU ARE FOOL ENOUGH TO WANT TO REMAIN A WOMAN.

YES!

I HATE YOU!
I KNOW, MY DEAR, AND I HATE YOU, TOO.

BY THE SAINTS, I AM WEARY UNTO THE BONE

WELL, SUMMON YOUR STRENGTH FOR ONE LIFE MORE, MY LADY.

IN VERY SOOTH? COULD IT NOT WAIT UPON THE MORROW?

THE NIGHT IS YOUNG, LADY. I GIVE YOU WHAT YOU CAME HERE SEEKING.

NOW, GAZE DEEP INTO MY BEING, AS I GAZED INTO YOURS.

The Tale of Queen Morgan
Midsummer Eve at Tintagel Castle. Gorlois, Duke of Cornwall, welcomes the birth of his second daughter…
DAMN IT TO HELL, WOMAN! YE'VE DROPPED ANOTHER BITCH! WHAT USE ARE YE IF YE CAN'T GIVE ME AN HEIR?
WAAAAAAAAHAAAAAAAAA WAAAAAAA
Thus is set the tone and content of a life-long relationship.

An exchange of familial sentiment...
WHICH ONE ARE YOU?
I AM MORGAN, FATHER.
NONE O' THAT! IT'S "MY LORD" IF YE'RE BIDDEN SPEAK AT ALL! HAS YER BITCH OF A MOTHER TAUGHT YE NAUGHT?
HOW OLD ARE YOU?
I AM SIX... "MY LORD."
GET YE BACK T' YER QUARTERS AND STAY THERE. YE'RE WORTHLESS FOR SIX YEARS YET.

A joyous and fortuitous occasion...
St Ives
WELL, THAT'S ONE DOWN. WHAT'S THE WENCH'S NAME AGAIN?
THINE ELDEST CHILD'S NAME IS MORGAUSE... MY LORD.

WELL, SHE'S LOT'S WIFE NOW, AND QUEEN OF ORKNEY.
THE DOWRY COST ME ENOUGH, BUT LOT WILL BE AN ALLY AGAINST PENDRAGON
WHO'S THIS ONE?
MORGAN... MY LORD.

HOW OLD IS SHE?
ELEVEN... MY LORD.
GOD'S BLOOD! WORTHLESS A TWELVE-MONTH YET!

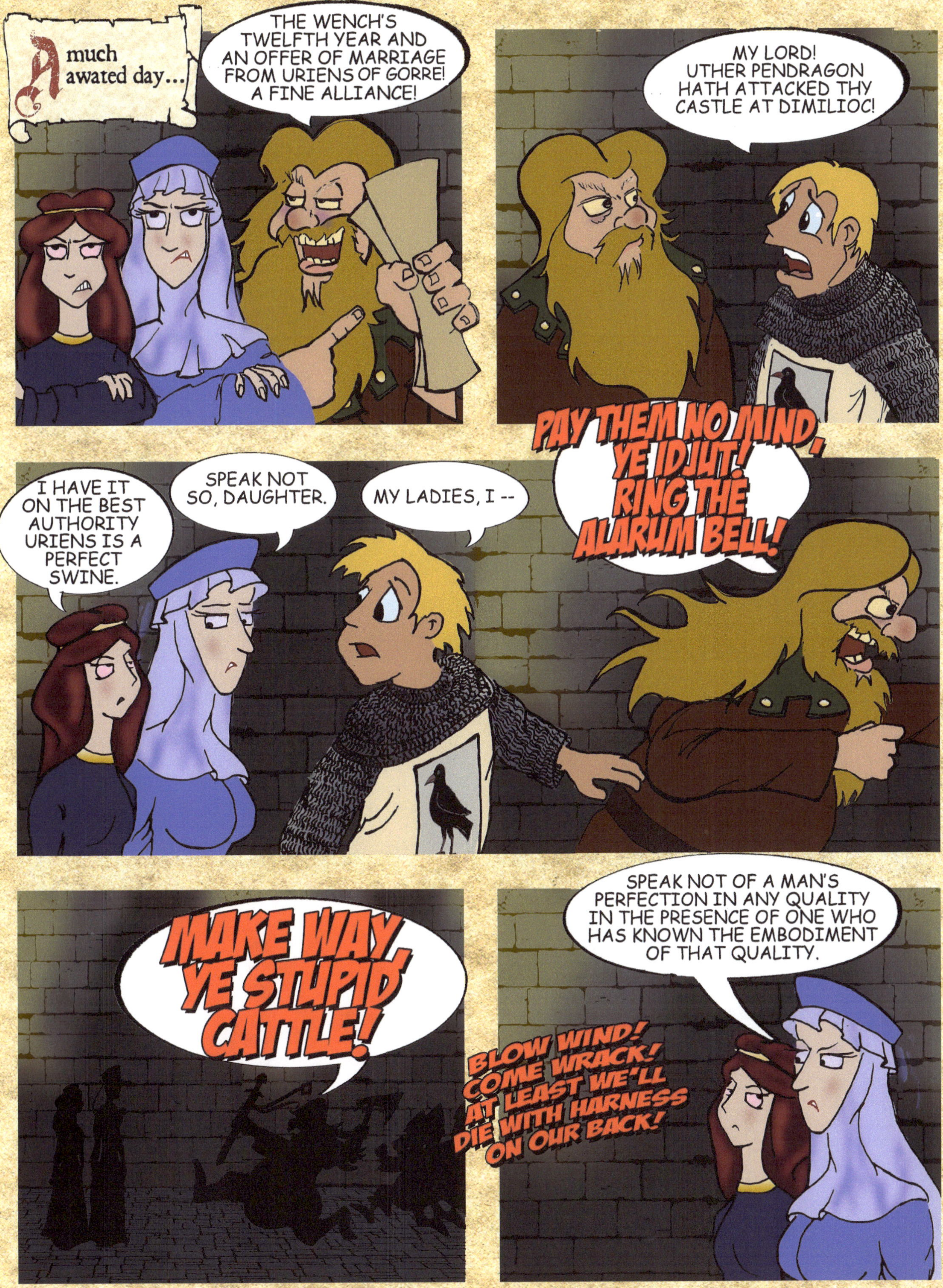

A much awated day...

THE WENCH'S TWELFTH YEAR AND AN OFFER OF MARRIAGE FROM URIENS OF GORRE! A FINE ALLIANCE!

MY LORD! UTHER PENDRAGON HATH ATTACKED THY CASTLE AT DIMILIOC!

I HAVE IT ON THE BEST AUTHORITY URIENS IS A PERFECT SWINE.

SPEAK NOT SO, DAUGHTER.

MY LADIES, I --

PAY THEM NO MIND, YE IDJUT! RING THE ALARUM BELL!

Vespers

RIDE, YE DOGS! IF I DON'T BREAK MY FAST ON PENDRAGON'S BALLOCKS, I'LL HAVE YERS!

Compline
WHO APPROACHES?
ARR! ME LORD GORLOIS! WE WARN'T EXPECTIN' YE. ERM.. HOW GOES THE BATTLE?
WELL, SIRRAH, WELL. PENDRAGON HATH LEFT THE FIELD.

I DO RETURN THAT I MIGHT SHARE MY JOY WITH MY BELOVED LADY!
errm... Aye... Milord.

JORY! 'AVE 'E EVER 'EARD THE LIKE FROM 'IM?
NAY JAGO! AN' DID 'E SEE THAT SMILE? BLOODY 'IDEOUS!

A reunion...
"FATHER"...

MORGAN, MY DEAREST! VICTORY IS OURS! I' HAVE COME BACK TO SHARE MY JOY WITH THY SWEET MOTHER!

GNNUMPH! I AM SURE SHE WILL BE AS SURPISED AS I!

IT IS A WISE CHILD...
(YOU MAY BE A VAST I'MPROVEMENT, BUT YOU ARE NOT MY FATHER.)

A WISE CHILD INDEED!

I DON'T BELIEVE I KNOW YOU.

NO, MY DEAR, I DON'T BELIEVE YOU DO... BUT YOU SHALL.

BUT FOR NOW, WISE CHILD...

ADIEU!
FOOM

A SORCEROR!

...AND AN INSUFFERABLY SMUG SORCEROR AT THAT "WISE CHILD" INDEED!. ... IT IS A WISE CHILD THAT KNOWS IT'S OWN...

GASP

MOTHER!

MOTHER! I MUST SPEAK WITH YOU!
WHAM WHAM WHAM WHAM WHAM

PLEASE STOP THAT, MY DEAREST. (NO, NOT YOU.) MORGAN, MOTHER IS VERY (GASP!) BUSY!

MOTHER, DO YOU KNOW WHO-

YES, I... YES... YES... YES! YES! YES!

YES! YES! YES!
OH, YES!
Yes!!

PRIME

I DO **HEAR** THINE EYES UPON ME, CHILD. GIVE THY THOUGHTS WORDS ERE THOU BURST.

THAT MAN WAS NOT MY FATHER!
BY THE SAINTS. MOTHER, IF I HEAR THOSE WORDS AGAIN --
WISE CHILD.
MY LADY IGERNE!

I GRIEVE TO TELL YOU THAT MY LORD GORLOIS WAS SLAIN LAST NIGHT AT DIMILIOC!

Oh, would I had known ere I had donned a red dress.

ERM... METHINKS I'D BEST RETRIEVE WHAT IS LEFT OF HIS LORDSHIP...
MOTHER, HOW CAN YOU SPEAK LIKE THAT? HE WAS YOUR HUSBAND!

MY CHILD, I DID LOVE HIM AS MUCH AS THOU DIDST.

WHICH WAS NOT AT ALL. AND THE FEELING WAS MUTUAL. BUT HE WAS A HUMAN BEING -AND MY FATHER!

THE FORMER IS DEBATABLE AND THE LATTER UNTRUE. GORLOIS WAS NOT THY FATHER.

HE WASN'T?

WAIT. HE WASN'T?

Think not, even for an instant, child, that I would ever bear progeny to such as Gorlois of Cornwall. Upon a night when Gorlois was joyfully slaking his bloodthirst, I called upon Arawn, king of the realm of Annwn, a lord of magic, death, and dark wisdom. With a right good will did he hie unto me.
And thus was my Morgan gotten.
My father was a Fairy?
Aye, child, and my mother, thy grandam as well.
Is my life about to change, Mother?
Aye, daughter.
I had a feeling it might.

Lord Amalud and the Green Lady
or The Getting of Duchess Igerne Part the First

Lord Amalud's a hunting gone
To chase the buck and doe.
With his good greyhounds and his bow of yew,
Right merrily he did go.

He had not gone a mile but two,
A mile or nearly three,
When in the clearing in the woods,
A wonder he did see.

Before him stood a snow-white hart
With horns of finest gold,
And round his neck he bore a crown.
A wonder to behold.

Lord Amalud reached for his bow.
The hart, he gave a leap.
And he and Amalud bounded forth
Into the forest deep.

And in that forest dark and green,
He rode an hour or more,
But never hart was to be seen,
Which grieved Amalud sore.

And then the air with music filled:
Lord Amalud silent fell.
The pipes and shawm and rebec trilled,
And dancers filled the dell.

Upon his horse he sits and gapes.
A troop of maids he sees
Who trip with galliards, jigs, and japes
So lightly through the trees.

And lo! A lady forth did come
Among the dancers there.
Amalud gazed as one struck dumb.
He'd ne'er seen maid so fair.

Her dress of green as young spring grass,
Yet green her visage rare.
Her eyes, they were as green as glass:
Likewise her wings and hair.

Amalud lept from off his horse
And knelt upon his knee.
'All hail thou mighty Queen of Heav'n!
Thy like I ne'er did see!'

'Arise! Arise, Lord Amalud,
Though, in faith, thy words are kind,
Had not so many called me thus,
I'd swear that thou wert blind!'

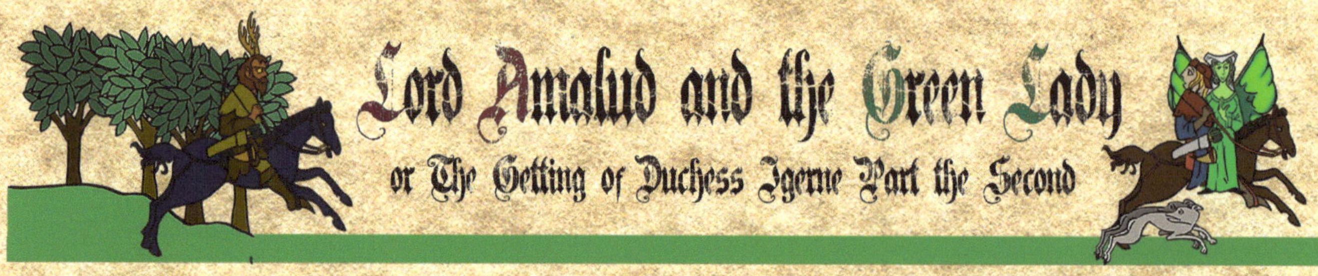

Lord Amalud and the Green Lady

or The Getting of Duchess Igerne Part the Second

"O Lady fair," said Amalud
"Come ride along with me,
Unto my castle we shall wend
And tomorrow wedded be.

Upon his horse the Lady sat.
They rode a quiet while.
Lord Amalud gazed into her eyes
And matched her, smile to smile.

They had not gone a mile or so,
A mile but barely one:
He looked and saw a rider come
From out the setting sun.

On they rode toward the east,
And darkness dimmed the skies.
Amalud turned his head and saw
The rider's glowing eyes.

The moon rose, and still on they rode.
Amalud gave a moan.
The rider rode in the full moon's glare.
His stag horns brightly shone.

"O Lady, Lady, tell me sooth!
I fear the dark one's wrath!
Is that the foe of all mankind
That follows in our path?"

"Thou spoke him once, My own true love.
It grieves my heart full sore.
If thou bespeak him once again,
Thou'lt never see me more."

And Amalud and the Lady wed,
Who in new shape was seen.
Her wings were gone. Her skin and hair
Had lost their former green.

And heavy soon with child was she.
A bonny girlchild born,
But came she not unto the font,
Upon the christening morn.

And thus Igerne christened was.
The vicar blessed the child,
But Amalud was filled with wrath.
His mien grew hot and wild.

"Why came ye not unto the kirk
To hear your own child named?
Before highborn and common folk
My family has been shamed!

I trow thou went unto the wood
Where thou wast lately queen,
And with the hornèd man thou went
To sport this day, I ween!"

The wrath then flashed in her green eyes.
Her wings, they sprouted new.
Before his eyes, her skin and hair
Regained their former hue.

"Lord Amalud, you were fair warned:
You spoke him once before.
Again you speak of the Forest Lord.
Look to see me no more."

Lord Amalud, he holds his child.
Now motherless is she.
The Lady of the forest green
He never more shall see.

In mystical Brocéliande
There dwells a lady fair.
Her eyes are green as finest glass,
Likewise her wings and hair.

She and her hornèd consort rule
The greenwood, deep and wild,
But oft times leave the woods to bear
Or sire a mortal child.

And thus throughout the mortal world
Are kinfolk of the wood,
And through many a mortal heart
Run steams of Fairy blood.

THE LADY OF BROCÉLIANDE IS THY GRANDAM?
NOTHING GETS PAST YOU, DOES IT? FOCUS.
ARE YOU BITTER?
THY GRANDSIRE, LORD AMALUD, DID MARRY ME OFF TO GORLOIS AS SOON AS DECENCY ALLOWED.
NOT UPON THIS MORROW, CHILD. BOTH ROT IN HELL, AND I BEAR THE SEED OF A KING WITHIN ME.
CONGRATULATIONS. I THOUGHT THAT MIGHT HAVE BEEN UTHER PENDRAGON VISITING YOU LAST NIGHT.
HA! A WISE CHILD, INDEED!
THE SUPERCILIOUS WIZARD WAS A DEAD GIVEAWAY. BUT IF YOU KNEW THAT WAS UTHER, WAS THE SHAPE-SHIFTING REALLY NECESSARY?
'TWAS THE WIZARD'S PLAN. IT DID ALLAY THE GUARDS' SUSPICION AND DOTH MAKE A GOOD TALE.
A PLAGIARISTIC TALE, IF YOU ASK ME. IT SOUNDS LIKE THE BEGETTING OF HERCULES..
THOU READST TOO MUCH.
WHY DO WE CARE HOW GOOD A TALE IT MAKES?
AH, WHY INDEED?
YOU ARE CRYPTIC, MOTHER.
THOU ART PEDANTIC, CHILD.
DO YOU LOVE UTHER?
WE DO NOT DO WHAT WE DO FOR LOVE.
YOU REALIZE I AM ONLY TWELVE. YOU ARE NOT EVEN TRYING TO BE A PROPER ROLE MODEL.
THOU'RT PRECOCIOUS. AND THOU SHALT KNOW HOW PROPER A MODEL I BE WHEN THOU KNOWST THY ROLE.

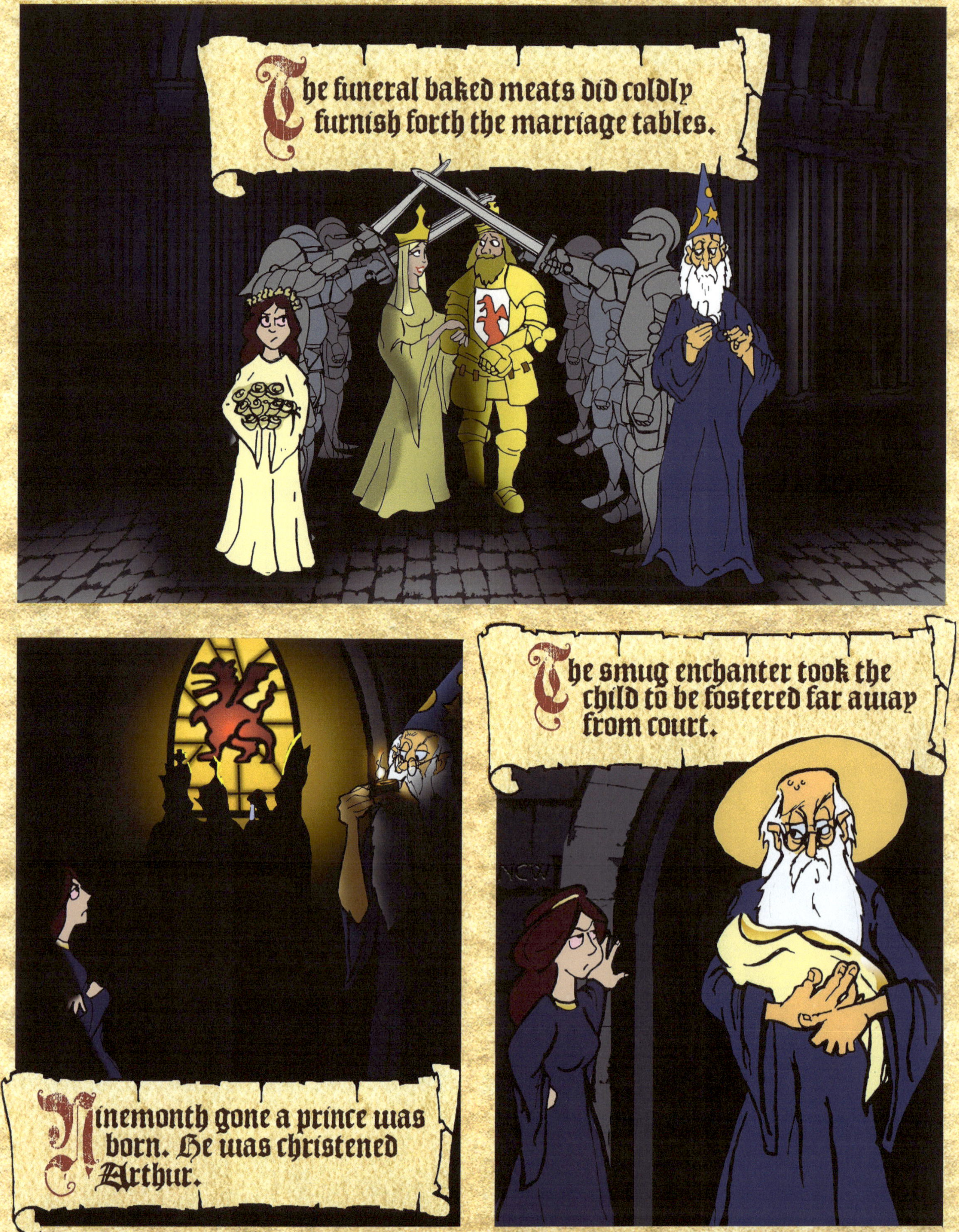

The funeral baked meats did coldly furnish forth the marriage tables.

FOOM

I DARE SAY THAT WOULD BE ADVISABLE.
SO... I SUPPOSE WE ARE GOING TO HAVE A LITTLE TALK.

MAY I SAFELY ASSUME THAT I SHALL RECEIVE A REASONABLE EXPLANATION FOR ALL THE UNNECESARY SUBTERFUGE AND CLASSICAL ALLUSION?
YOU MAY INDEED, MY LADY. AND I MUST SAY WHAT A PLEASURE IT IS TO CONVERSE WITH A YOUNG PERSON WHO IS AS OSTENTATIOUSLY AND PEDANTICALLY VERBOSE AS MYSELF!

ZOINK!
AND, INDEED, I RECEIVED A SATISFACTORY EXPLANATION. AND SIX MONTHS LATER, I WAS MARRIED OFF TO URIENS OF GORRE. I WAS NOT HAPPY ABOUT IT, BUT IT HAD TO BE.

AND THE EXPLANATION?
THAT IS PART OF WHY YOU ARE HERE IN THE FIRST PLACE. BUT YOU MUST BE WEARY. I SHALL CALL MISTRESS CAILLIC TO SHOW YOU TO YOUR QUARTERS.

I HAVE LIVED A THOUSAND LIVES THIS DAY.

I HAVE SEEN THE GETTING OF A KING AND TWO QUEENS. I HAVE LEARNED MUCH.

AND YET.. FOR ALL I HAVE SEEN AND HEARD AND DONE THIS NIGHT, I KNOW NOTHING.

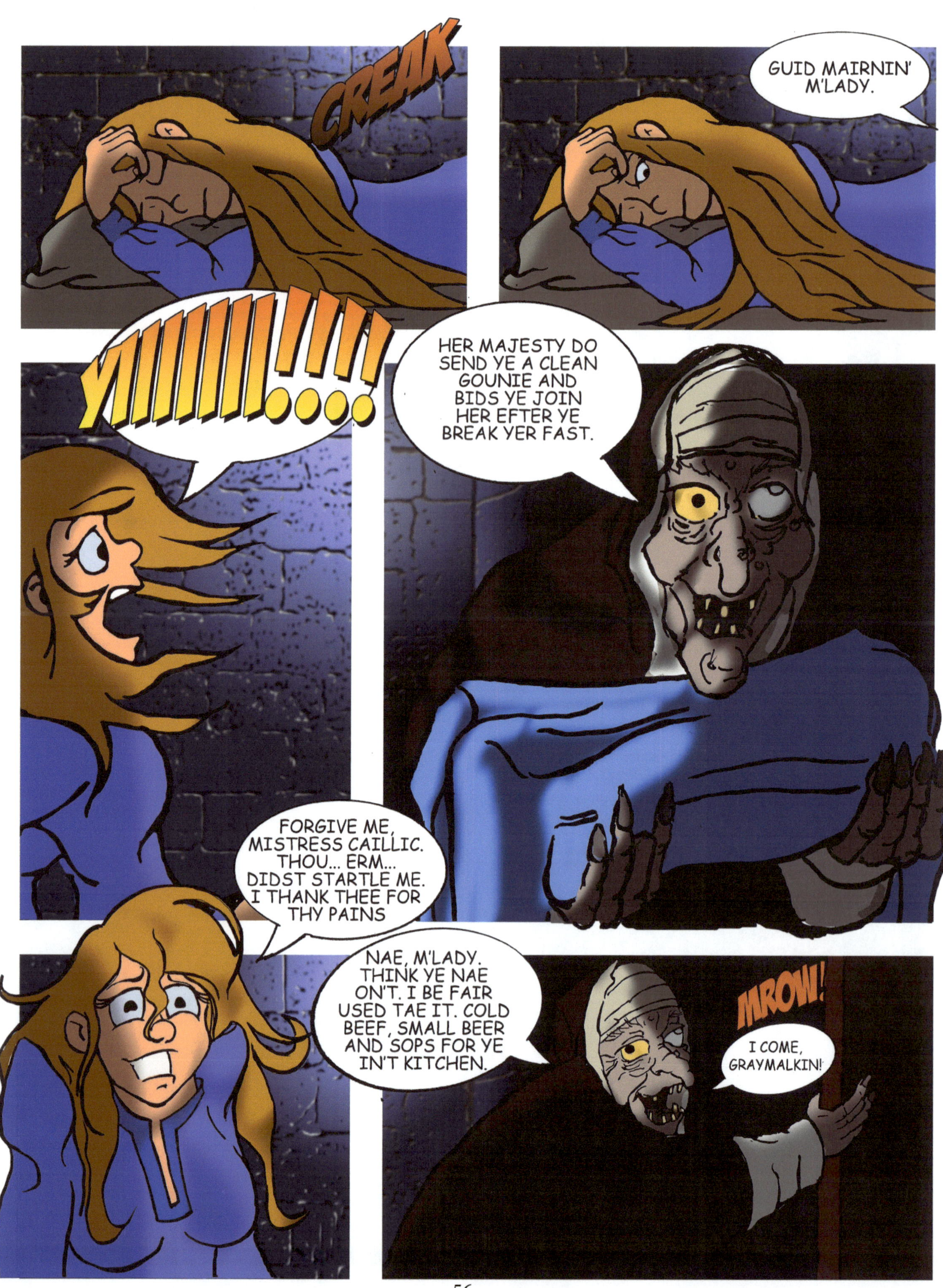
CREAK
GUID MAIRNIN' M'LADY.
YIIIIIII!!!!....
HER MAJESTY DO SEND YE A CLEAN GOUNIE AND BIDS YE JOIN HER EFTER YE BREAK YER FAST.
FORGIVE ME, MISTRESS CAILLIC. THOU... ERM... DIDST STARTLE ME. I THANK THEE FOR THY PAINS
NAE, M'LADY. THINK YE NAE ON'T. I BE FAIR USED TAE IT. COLD BEEF, SMALL BEER AND SOPS FOR YE IN'T KITCHEN.
MROW!
I COME, GRAYMALKIN!

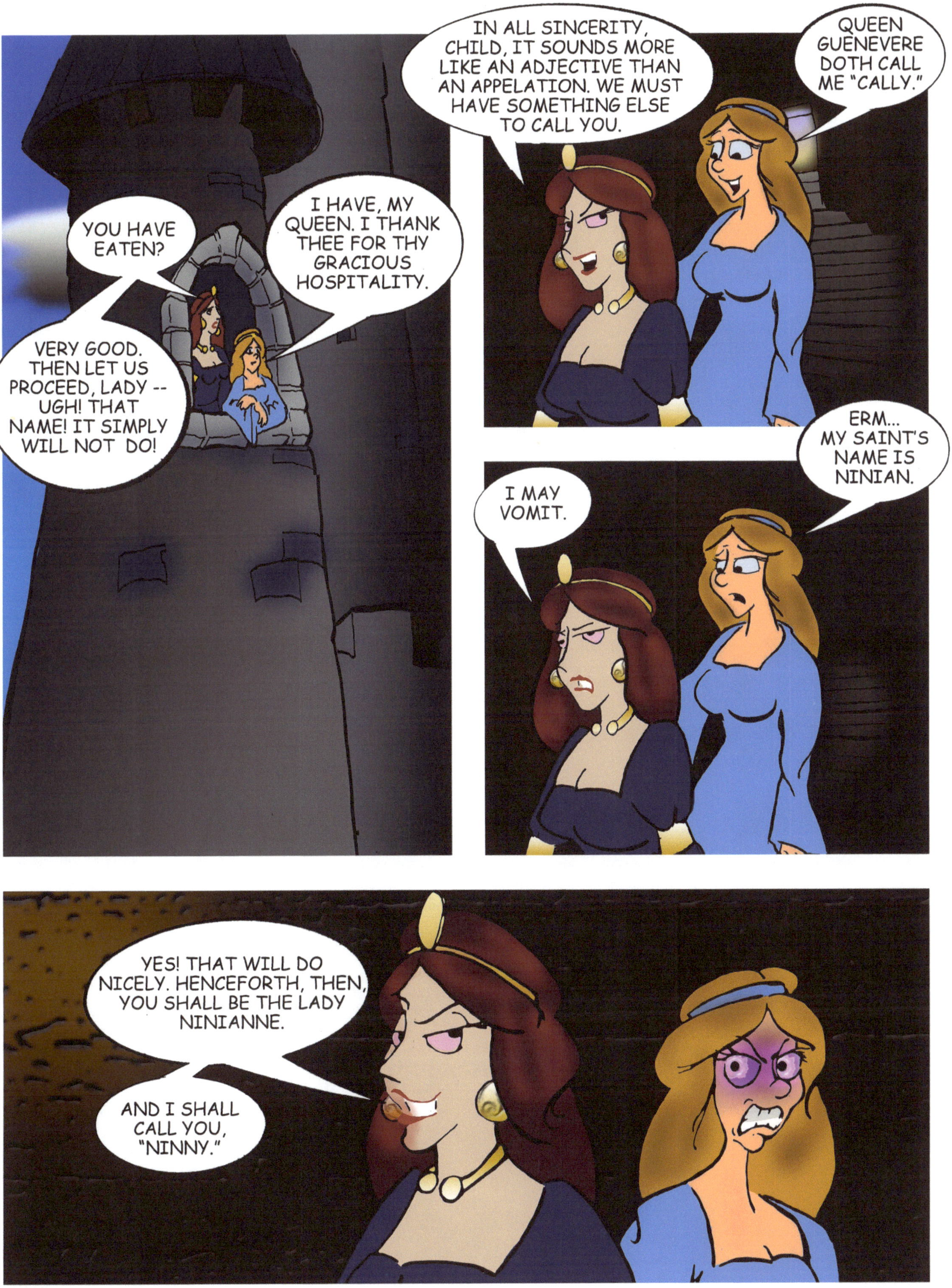

YOU HAVE EATEN?

I HAVE, MY QUEEN. I THANK THEE FOR THY GRACIOUS HOSPITALITY.

VERY GOOD. THEN LET US PROCEED, LADY -- UGH! THAT NAME! IT SIMPLY WILL NOT DO!

IN ALL SINCERITY, CHILD, IT SOUNDS MORE LIKE AN ADJECTIVE THAN AN APPELATION. WE MUST HAVE SOMETHING ELSE TO CALL YOU.

QUEEN GUENEVERE DOTH CALL ME "CALLY."

ERM... MY SAINT'S NAME IS NINIAN.

I MAY VOMIT.

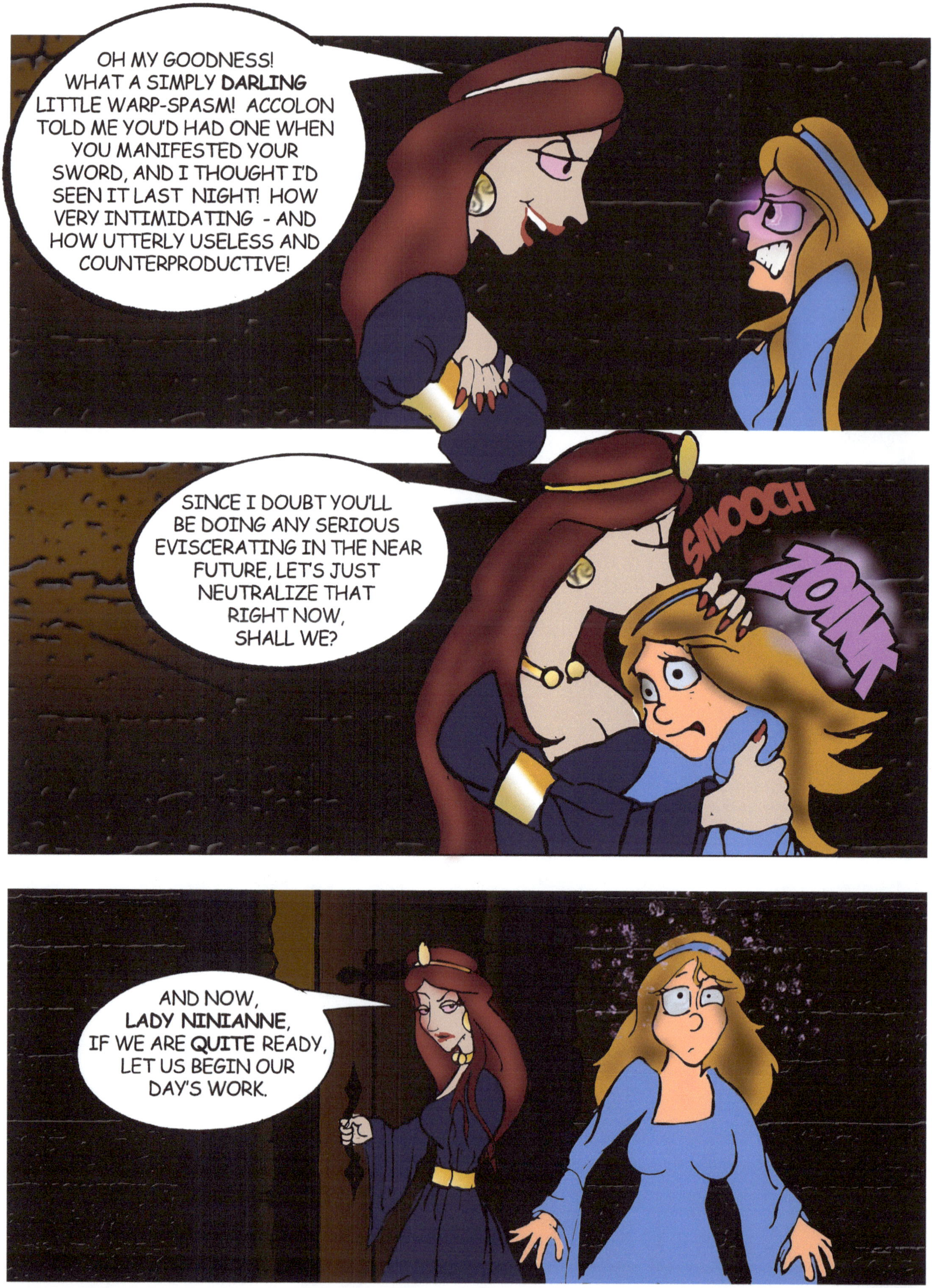

OH MY GOODNESS! WHAT A SIMPLY **DARLING** LITTLE WARP-SPASM! ACCOLON TOLD ME YOU'D HAD ONE WHEN YOU MANIFESTED YOUR SWORD, AND I THOUGHT I'D SEEN IT LAST NIGHT! HOW VERY INTIMIDATING - AND HOW UTTERLY USELESS AND COUNTERPRODUCTIVE!

SINCE I DOUBT YOU'LL BE DOING ANY SERIOUS EVISCERATING IN THE NEAR FUTURE, LET'S JUST NEUTRALIZE THAT RIGHT NOW, SHALL WE?

SMOOCH

ZOINK

WE WILL HAVE TO WEAN YOU OFF THAT WARP SPASM.
CUCHULAIN OF ULSTER DID HAVE A WARP SPASM... AND HE WAS A HERO!
My lady, you may have lived the lives of a thousand women, but you are still thinking like those armored lummoxes back at Camelot. Warriors like Cuchulain are well and fine in their place, but ultimately the protruding eye, the muscles the size of babies' heads rolling up and down the arms, and that nine-cubit gush of blood make for a great show, but it's all so abominably messy and doesn't get the job done.
A well-worked spell or a well-placed assassin are far more effectve. No, warp spasms are not what you are about.
cuchulain
cuchulain in warp spasm
AND WHAT AM I ABOUT, MY QUEEN? AND WHAT DID MYRDDYN TELL THEE THAT NIGHT? AND WHAT GLAMOUR HAST THOU WORKED UPON MINE UNCLE THE KING?
THEN AGAIN, THERE ARE TIMES WHEN A WARP SPASM IS PARTICULARLY GRATIFYING..

THIS IS WHAT YOU ARE ABOUT, MY LADY.
PLOCK!
IT IS THE AWEN. THE BARDS AND DRUIDS CALL IT THE FIRE IN THE HEAD. IT IS THE FLAME OF INSPIRATION, AND IT IS THE SOURCE OF YOUR POWER.

THROUGH YOUR MIND AND SOUL RUNS THE SPIRAL OF TIME AND SPACE. WITHIN YOU ARE THE POWERS OF MAKING AND TRANSFORMATION. YOU ARE A FORMER AND A SHAPER.

THE AWEN IS WITHIN AND WITHOUT. BEFORE YOU IS THE VORTEX OF TIME AND SPACE, AND THE AWEN SHALL BE YOUR ENTRY AND YOUR GUIDE...
ZOINK
...IF YOU EVER LEARN TO CONTROL IT.

USE THE POWER OF YOUR AWEN TO SUMMON THAT FLAGON.

PWINK

PONDERING UPON THE FLAGON DID GIVE ME A THIRST.

LESSONS PROGRESS APACE...
ONCE MORE, I CANNOT STRESS ENOUGH THE VITAL IMPORTANCE OF CLEAR AND EXACT PRONUNCIATION.

LEARNING IS NOT CHILD'S PLAY; WE CAN NOT LEARN WITHOUT PAIN.
-- ARISTOTLE
JUST A FEW MORE CORE TEXTS. WE SHALL GO OVER THE COMMENTARIES AFTER WE SUP.

EXTEND THE AWEN, FIX UPON YOUR DESTINATION, AND TRY NOT TO LAND IN A WALL THIS TIME.
THE ROOTS OF EDUCATION ARE BITTER, BUT THE FRUIT IS SWEET.
-- ARISTOTLE
FOOM

FOOM

FOOM

CONCENTRATE. PORK PIE BECOMES HEDGEHOG.
ANYONE CAN MAKE MISTAKES, BUT ONLY AN IDIOT PERSISTS IN ERROR.
--MARCUS TULLIUS CICERO
MURBLE MURBLE MURBLE
FWUMP
SNARL
NOT BAD, ACTUALLY, BUT MAKE A NOTE TO AVOID MISTRESS MATHONWY'S RAREBIT BEFORE CONJURING...
FWUMP
PLOP

AFTER MUCH TRIAL & EVEN MORE ERROR...
LADY NINIANNE, YOU'VE SURPASSED MY EXPECTATIONS. WE HAVE REACHED THE PENULTIMATE LESSON IN OUR TUTELAGE.

IT AWAITS YOU IN HERE.

WHAT IS IT THAT AWAITS ME, MY QUEEN?

SLAM
THAT WHICH YOU FEAR THE MOST!

CALOGRENANT!

CALOGRENANT!

THERE YE BE! GOD BE PRAISED!

WHAT DO YE IN THIS HEATHENISH PLACE?
GAWAIN! I -- *GASP* MY VOICE!
CAL! WHAT AILS YE LAD?
OH NO! OH, DEAR MOTHER!
NO!

UP, THEN, AND ON THY FEET!

LET"S HAE A LOOK AT THEE, LAD

I AM NOT A LAD!

NAY, CAL, INDEED THOU'RT NOT.. THOU ART A MAN - AND THE IMAGE O' THY FAITHER, REST TAE HIS SOUL.

NAY! I AM-- THIS CASTLE! THE MAIDEN--

CALOGRENANT, LOOK ABOUT THEE.

NAE CASTLE. NAE MAIDEN... NAE GOOD TAE THIS PLACE AS WELL. YE'VE A GLAMOUR ON YE, O' THAT I'M SURE. LET US BE GONE.
NO!
'TIS AN UNHOLY PLACE. PUTS ME IN MIND O' THE MOUND WHERE I DID MEET THE GREEN KNIGHT THAT WOULD HAVE MY HEAD.
AYE... A PLACE O' DREAMS AND DEVILTRY. 'TIS WELL I FOUND YE IN TIME. FOLLOW. THY HORSE IS WI' MINE...
NO!
NO! NO! NO! NO!
!
NO.

A WORD, SIR GAWAIN?
AYE, SIR CALOGRENANT?
WHERE IS THY BELT?
BELT SAY YE?
THOU HAST SAID IT. THE GREEN KNIGHT, SIR BERCILAK, DID CHALLENGE THEE TO EXCHANGE BLOWS AND THOU WERT HONOR-BOUND TO RECEIVE A BLOW OF HIM . THOU DIDST STAY THREE DAYS IN HIS CASTLE, THOUGH THOU KNEW NOT. LADY BERCILAK GAVE THEE A GREEN BELT THAT WOULD RENDER THEE INVULNERABLE, AND THOU DIDST ACCEPT IT. FOR WANTING TO PROTECT THYSELF, WHICH ANY HUMAN WOULD DO, SIR BERCILAK GAVE THEE BUT A NICK, BUT THOU WERT ASHAMED AT THY COWARDICE. SINCE THAT DAY, IT WAS EVER ON THY ARMOR TO SPUR THY HUMILITY. WHERE IS THY GREEN BELT, SIR GAWAIN?*
* Sir Gawain and the Green Knight
SIR ACCOLON, THOU ART FORTUNATE TO BE STILL IN ONE PIECE.
MY LADY, THOU ART FAIR PERCEPTIVE.

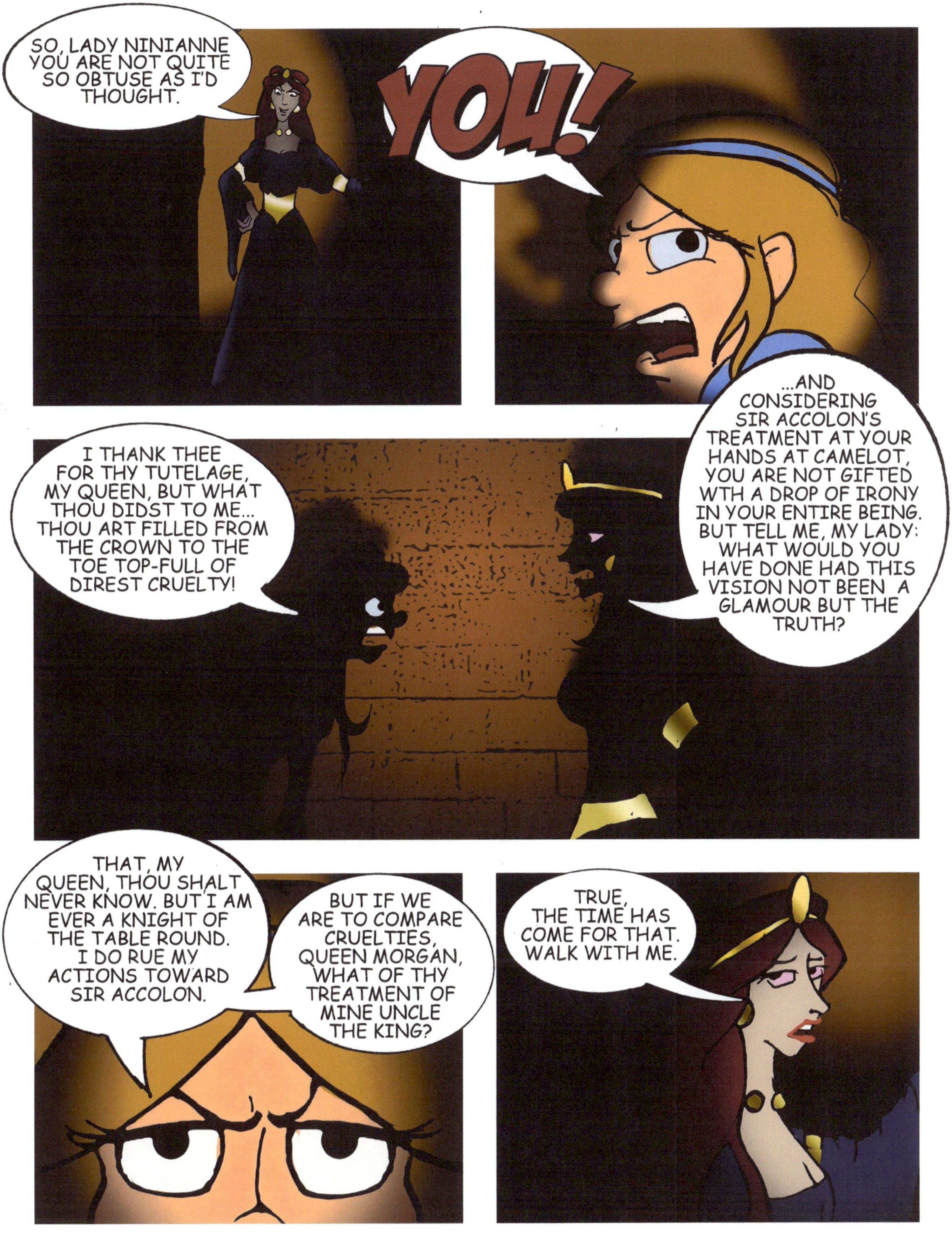

SO, LADY NINIANNE YOU ARE NOT QUITE SO OBTUSE AS I'D THOUGHT.

YOU!

I THANK THEE FOR THY TUTELAGE, MY QUEEN, BUT WHAT THOU DIDST TO ME... THOU ART FILLED FROM THE CROWN TO THE TOE TOP-FULL OF DIREST CRUELTY!

...AND CONSIDERING SIR ACCOLON'S TREATMENT AT YOUR HANDS AT CAMELOT, YOU ARE NOT GIFTED WTH A DROP OF IRONY IN YOUR ENTIRE BEING. BUT TELL ME, MY LADY: WHAT WOULD YOU HAVE DONE HAD THIS VISION NOT BEEN A GLAMOUR BUT THE TRUTH?

I, ON THE OTHER HAND, KNOW HIM. I HAVE SHARED HIS BED AND BORNE HIM CHILDREN. THERE IS NOT ONE WHIT OF HIS LIFE TO WHICH I HAVE NOT BEEN PRIVY.

LOVE WAS NOT A BARGAINING CHIP IN THIS UNION, AND IT WAS NEITHER OFFERED NOR GIVEN. HONOR HIM? I HAVE KNOWN HIM TOO LONG.

AS SISTER TO THE HIGH KING, I WAS, TO HIS MIND, A VALUABLE HOSTAGE.

AS WIFE TO ONE OF THE STRONGEST VASSAL KINGS IN THE NORTH, I WAS IN A FAVORABLE POSITION TO DO MY... WORK. IT WAS A CIVIL, SYMBIOTIC RELATIONSHIP - AT LEAST UNTIL THREE YEARS AGO, ABOUT THE TIME YOU HAD GONE TO ARTHUR'S COURT, WHEN I HEARD HIM SPEAK SECRETLY WITH TWO SAXON ENVOYS, WHO PROMISED HIM SOVEREIGNTY OVER ALL THE NORTH IF HE AIDED THEM IN AN INVASION AND INSURRECTION.

Needless to say, the Saxons did not return with King Uriens' answer. Indeed, they did not make it past the moat. But King Uriens was another problem entirely. He could not be trusted and was a danger to the kingdom of Britain, but his disgrace would destroy the family and give other vassal kings reason to snatch the crown from my chidren.
Yet I would not kill him outright.

...SO THE HARMONY OF THE LAND WAS SECURED WHEN I RELIEVED THE KING OF HIS WITS AND WHAT WAS LEFT OF HIS YOUTH. TRUST ME. ALL OF GORRE IS HAPPIER THIS WAY - KING URIENS INCLUDED.

THOU... THOU DIDST ACT FOR THE SAKE OF THE LAND. THOU ART LOYAL TO THY BROTHER, KING ARTHUR. BUT THE QUEEN DOTH SAY--
A BAD REPUTATION IS A VERY USEFUL THING FOR ONE WHO DEALS REGULARLY WITH THE DARK. AND THE BAD JUDGMENT OF YOUR PRETTY COUSIN SHALL BE SUNG BY BARDS FOR CENTURIES.

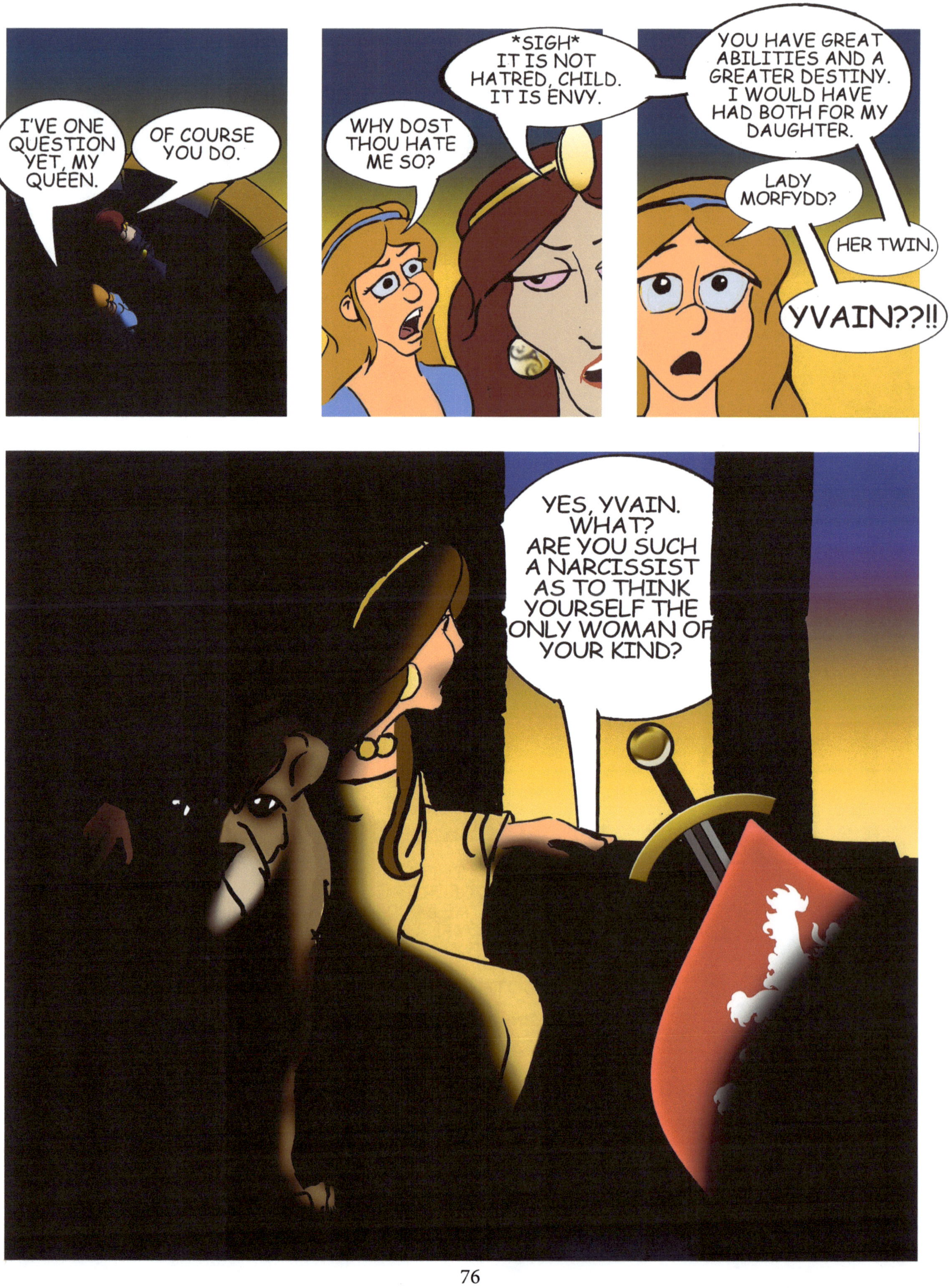

YES, YVAIN. WHAT? ARE YOU SUCH A NARCISSIST AS TO THINK YOURSELF THE ONLY WOMAN OF YOUR KIND?

SOME YEARS AGO SHE RETURNED FROM A QUEST WITH THAT DAMNED LION OF HERS IN TOW.

SHE CONFIDED IN ME REGARDING HER TRUE NATURE. IN TRUTH, I WAS MORE SURPRISED THAT SHE'D FOUND A LION IN BRITAIN THAN THAT SHE WAS POSSESSED OF A FEMALE SOUL.

WE HAD HOPES. A WOMAN OF HER KIND WOULD BE GIFTED WITH A GREAT AWEN, WOULD BE TRANSFORMED, AND WOULD SERVE THE LAND... AND MORE. BUT MY POWERS WERE NOT SUCH AS TO CREATE SUCH A METAMORPHOSIS IN HER
NO. IT WAS YOU FROM THE START. NOT MY POOR GIRL. IT WAS FORTUNATE THAT I'D WROUGHT THAT SMALL CHANGE IN HER FATHER, OR SHE WOULD BE DEAD. SHE IS SAFE HERE WITH ACCOLON, MY LADIES, AND ME.

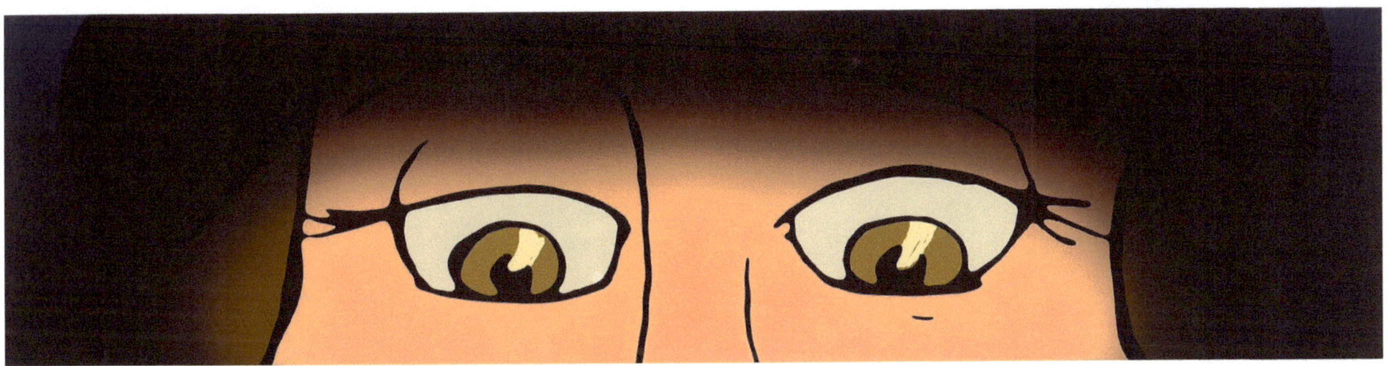

I HAVE HEARD ENOUGH, MY QUEEN.

YANK
MY QUEEN, IF THOU WOULDST FORGIVE THE PRESUMPTION...

DEAR COZ, A MOMENT...
NAB
WHOOSH!

MISTRESS CAILLIC, WE HAVE NEED OF THEE.
ANON, MILADY!
EYE OF NEWT

LADY NINIANNE, YOU ARE BECOMING ARROGANT, OVERBEARING AND SMUG.
I DO BUT EMULATE MY MENTORS.
UNDERSTOOD, NONETHELESS...

ODD. I DON'T REMEMBER THIS.
I DID BUILD IT AS WE WALKED HERE.
INDEED? POINTS FOR STYLE AND INITIATIVE,

WELL?
OCH, AN' A FAIR LOVELY WELL IT IS, TOO. IS THAT NAE SO, YER HIGHNESS?

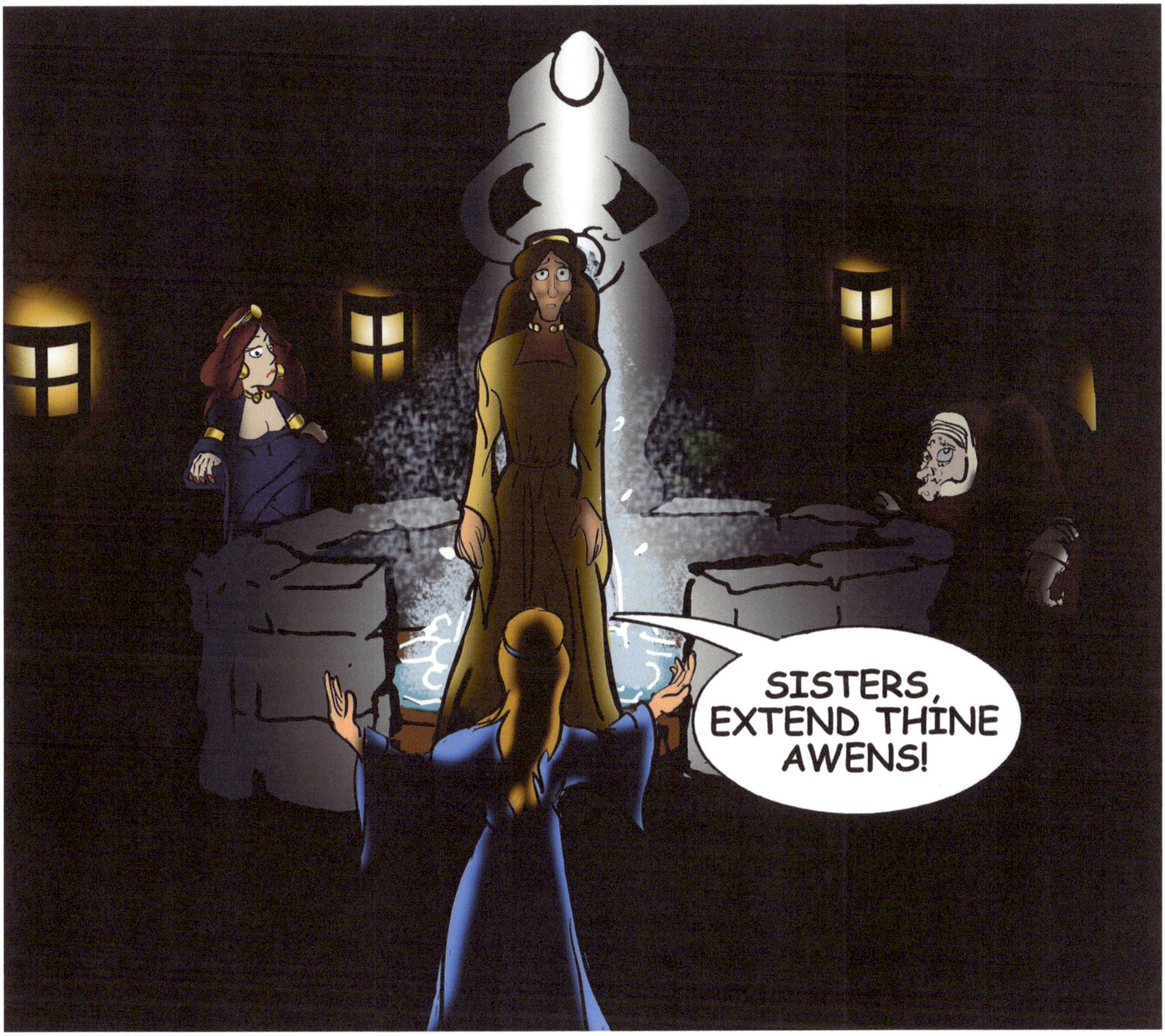

SISTERS, EXTEND THINE AWENS!

the Awen

O beloved daughter! With joy I claim thee as mine own!

And lo! I infuse thee with my spirit!

FLUMP!

IF SHE HAS DIED, I SWEAR BY MY DARK FATHER --
NAY, NAY, YER MAJESTY, DINNA FASH YERSEL'. MY LADY DO BUT SLEEP.

I DO NOT RECALL TEACHING YOU ANY SUCH CONJURATION OF THIS NATURE, **LADY NINIANNE**
I HAVE BEEN A THOUSAND WOMEN, MY QUEEN. I HAVE SEEN MUCH AND LEARNED FROM IT.
MY LADY WAKES.

HMPH! FOR ALL THE GOOD IT HAS DONE! MY POOR GIRL HAS NOT CHANGED AT ALL.

NAY, MOTHER! I HAVE BEEN TRANSFORMED! I AM A DAUGHTER OF THE GREAT MOTHER! MY WOMANHOOD IS NO THING OF PALTRY FLESH! IT IS A THING OF THE SPIRIT AND SOUL - OR IF IT BE CORPOREAL, IT IS SUCH THAT FILLS ME FROM TOP TO TOE WITH MY DIVINE MOTHER'S ESSENCE. NEVER MORE SHALL I GIVE THROUGHT TO THE JIBES OF AN IGNORANT WORLD, FOR THE GREAT MOTHER DWELLS IN ME AND I IN HER.

YOU HAVE LEARNED WELL AND WEILD YOUR POWERS IMPRESSIVELY. YOU REMIND ME OF ME -- WHICH ANNOYS ME NO END.

I HAVE SEEN THE MOTHER AND FELT HER LOVE!
EEEE! THA' WERE FUN! WHEN SHA' WE THREE MEET AGAIN, IN THUNDER, LIGHTNIN' OR IN RAIN?
ASK HER.

ARE YOU COMING?
ANON, MY QUEEN. I'VE BUSINESS YET.

MOTHER?
YES, MY CHILD?
AUTHORIAL INTRUSION...
LIKE MANY ARTHURIAN CHARACTERS, YVAIN AND URIENS WERE HISTORICAL. ACCORDING TO THE LEGEND OF ST KENTIGERN, YVAIN BEGOT ST. KENTIGERN, APOSTLE OF STRATHCLYDE. UPON TANEU, DAUGHTER OF KING LOT OF LOTHIAN, WHILE IN THE GARB OF A WOMAN. HISTORIAN ADAM ARDREY, IN HIS BOOK *FINDING MERLIN*, SUGGESTS THAT SINCE THERE WAS NO NEED FOR DISGUISE, YVAIN MAY HAVE BEEN A TRANS-WOMAN. TENUOUS? YES, BUT IT WORKS FOR ME.

HOW CAMEST THOU TO GUESS, MY CHILD?
'TWAS FAIR EASY, MY LADY.

I NEVER KNEW MY MOTHER, BUT THE TALE OF MY BEGETTING AND HER LEAVING SOUNDETH MUCH LIKE UNTO THAT OF QUEEN YGERNE.

METHINKETH I NEEDS MUST COMPOSE A NEW SCENARIO.
AND METHINKETH QUEEN MORGAN SHOULD HAVE MUCH TO SAY SHOULD SHE EVER LEARN I AM HER AUNT.

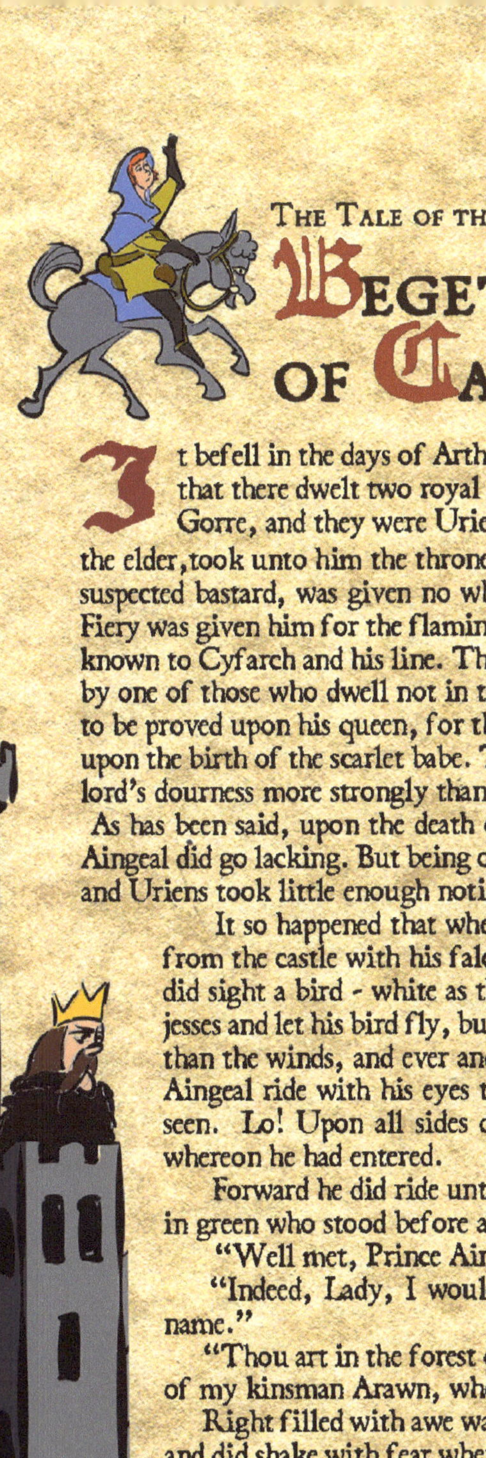

The Tale of the Begetting and Birth of Calogrenant

Part the first

It befell in the days of Arthur Pendragon, when he was but new-made king of Britain, that there dwelt two royal brothers in the North, sons of Cyfarch the Dour, King of Gorre, and they were Uriens and Aingeal. Upon the death of Cyfarch, Uriens, being the elder,took unto him the throne of Gorre. But Aingeal, being not only the younger, but suspected bastard, was given no whit of land. Indeed, his very name Aingeal which meaneth Fiery was given him for the flaming hair which did grace his head at birth – a colour then unknown to Cyfarch and his line. Thus Cyfach did suppose that he had been cuckolded, and that by one of those who dwell not in the sight of the Lord, a fairy or a daemon. It was, alas, not to be proved upon his queen, for the Maker of All saw fit to take her to Paradise or Perdition upon the birth of the scarlet babe. Thus Aingeal did dwell in the house of Cyfarch and felt my lord's dourness more strongly than many.

As has been said, upon the death of my lord Cyfarch, Uriens did ascend to the throne, and Aingeal did go lacking. But being of good and giving heart, Aigeal bore his brother no ill will, and Uriens took little enough notice of his brother that the two were at peace.

It so happened that when Aingeal did reach the age of twenty years, he rode forth from the castle with his falcon upon his wrist. Some way from his brother's castle, he did sight a bird - white as the snows but with the shape of a raven. Aingeal loosed the jesses and let his bird fly, but the white raven would not be stricken and anon flew faster than the winds, and ever and on did Aingeal's goshawk fly after. Through the day did Aingeal ride with his eyes to the heavens until he did find that no heavens were to be seen. Lo! Upon all sides did he see but forest green, nor could he discern the path whereon he had entered.

Forward he did ride until he came unto a clearing and here did he meet a maiden all in green who stood before a fountain and did greet him thus:

"Well met, Prince Aingeal! Thou art far from home, I ween."

"Indeed, Lady, I would know not only where I am but how thou knowest my name."

"Thou art in the forest of Brocéliande, and I am the lady of this land. Thou art son of my kinsman Arawn, whose dark lands lie close at hand."

Right filled with awe was Aingeal, for he had heard the name of that dark fairy lord and did shake with fear when the bards did tell of him. For many hours did he discourse with the Lady of Brocéliande, and he found her passing fair.

"Lady," said he, "I would have thee to wed, but it is to my shame that I have no lands of my own."

"Fie!" said she, "Go thou unto thy brother and ask of him for a plot of land to plant a garden, no more than can be covered by a boar's skin."

"Right willingly will he render that," saith Aingeal, "but what good might come to me of such a plot?"

Here the lady did smile, and in her smile was the beauty and the awfulness that lay in this world and in the realms beneath the earth.

"Be thou guided by me, my love, and thou shalt have thy land and thy lady.

The Tale of the Begetting and Birth of Calogrenant Part the Second

And so it passed that Aingeal went unto his brother the king and said unto him.

"My liege, I would beg of thee a small favor."

Uriens, who was right pleased that his brother should be beholden unto him, did smile and say, "Whatever thou dost ask shall be thine."

"I would have a small plot of land," sayeth Aingeal.

Uriens here lost his good will, for he was right parsimonious with the land his kingship had given unto him. "Land, thou sayst? How much wouldst thou have of me, brother?" sayeth Uriens.

"Only as much," sayeth Aingeal, "as can be encompassed by the skin of a boar."

Now did this Uriens laugh full heartily at the foolishness of his brother, for what might be done with such a pittance of land? Thus did the king grant his brother only so much land as a boar's skin might contain. And in his generosity granted that he might choose any place in the kingdom of Gorre.

Upon that very day did the Lady of Brocéliande appear unto Aingeal.

"And hast thou gotten thy brother the king's consent?"

"Aye, lady," sayeth Aingeal, "And I shall have my choice of any spot in the kingdom, but what will such a small tract avail me?"

The Lady of Brocéliande said naught but laughed a laugh that sounded like unto the running of waters. In a trice she hath transported Aingeal to that part of his brother's lands which was the riches with fields an forest. Aingeal stood amazed.

"Wouldst thou have this unto thyself, Aingeal? Wouldst thou then be worthy of such a lady as I?"

"Aye, lady. But I may have only the width and breadth of a boar's skin."

The Lady of Brocéliande smiled, and Aingeal found in his hands a well-made boar spear. While he marveled, he did hear a roar, and turning saw charging upon him a right monstrous boar, full twenty hands at the shoulder, with tusks that might kill a horse at a touch. Then did Aingeal sink onto one knee and brace his spear against the knee that touched the ground. The boar in his fury ran straight upon the spear up to the cross-piece, and lo! His heart doth cleave in twain.

"Well, " sayeth the Lady of Brocéliande, "thou hast thy boar. Now shalt thou have thy land.

Aingeal did marvel when the Lady brought forth from her sleeve a fine knife with a bone handle, and marveled he yet more when she fell to skinning the boar with more skill than any yeoman or woodsman he had known, so that in as long as a poet might take to say it, a skinless carcass and a fine boar's hide lay before him.

Then did the Lady of Brocéliande smile a smile of mischief. "We shall have thy land, my love,

And straight she fell to slitting of the boar's hide in strips as fine as silken thread, yet no break did she make in those strips. Aingeal did wonder to see the knife slit back and forth and the boar's skin grow thinner and thinner, and the lady take not a drop of blood upon herself.

When she had done, she sang a song with words Aingeal could not comprehend, and lo, there came unto the lady a multitude of tiny folk. Some had wings. Some, though seeming human, though small, were also like unto the beasts of the forest. All took a piece of the boar skin strand and pulled as far as it might go.

Again Aingeal marveled. For the boar skin encompassed five leagues in each direction.

"Thou hast it, My Love," sayeth the Lady of Brocéliande, who did smile upon him, "All the land which the boar's skin encompasseth is thine – as am I."

And when King Uriens did see this marvel, he was full of wrath, yet he was as good as his word. And Aingeal built him a fine castle, and he had many farms, and he had finer hunting than any place in the island of Britain. And he did dearly love his wife, the Lady of Brocéliande. But, alas, his brother King Uriens was now bitter and cold, and though he offered him no harm, neither was there love nor generosity in his heart for Aingeal until Aingeal left this world.

THE TALE OF THE

BEGETTING AND BIRTH OF CALOGRENANT PART THE THIRD

It happened not long thereafter that Aingeal and the Lady of Brocéliande were wed, and she the Lady became heavy with child. As she neared her time of birthing, she sayeth unto Aingeal, "My Lord Husband, though it may grieve thee sore, I must tell thee that the babe within me is a girl child."

Aingeal marveled much at his wife's speaking and sayeth unto her, "My Lady Wife, I do welcome this child with all my soul, whether a son or daughter it may be. But tell me in sooth: how canst thou be so assured in thy prophecy?"

The Lady smiled full knowingly. "I come of The Old People," sayeth she, "and so dost thou. There is much revealed to us to which Daughters of Eve and Sons of Adam are right blind. Nay! I shall tell thee more. The child within my womb shall grow to be a woman of great power and wisdom, and she shall be known to the bards of the ages." And Aingeal was right joyful at these tidings.

It came to pass, then, that The Lady was did go to her chamber with her maids, and the midwife was called for. Aingeal did wait in the hallway outside for many hours. At the strike of twelve he did doze by The Lady's chamber door when he espied a wonder, and right unwelcome was that which met his eyes. From out the dark – Nay! It seemeth out of the stones of the walls themselves did stride a man of regal bearing, robed in leather he was, with skin as brown as a walnut. But mark ye the stag horns he wears in the place of a crown! The daemon, or so he seemeth to be, trode toward The Lady's door. Aingeal did block his way, but the Horned Man did bare his teeth and fling Aingeal from out his path with but a flick of his arm. Then heard Aingeal angry voices and cries of dismay from his Lady's room. He did draw his sword and run to his Lady's side. The maids and midwife lay in a swoon. The Horned man was not to be seen, but the Lady of Brocéliande sat in bed a-nursing a new-born babe and weeping. "This child," cried she, "was to be a woman of power and greatness, "but the Lord of Brocéliande hath made it not so. His presence in my chamber hath made a boy child."

Much did Aingeal wonder at these words, but kept he his silence. Then did the Lady of Brocéliande rise from off the bed and place the babe in Aingeal's arms.

"Take thou this child," said she, "and raise him as thou seest fit. My words were for a girl child and not a male, yet this child's true form is female, and she shall know it in her heart and in her soul. Aingeal, thou hast done no wrong, but I free thee of thy bond to me. Marry whom thou wilt, and look to see me no more."

Before his eyes the Lady of Brocéliande did grow wings, and her countenance and hair did grow as green as her gown. Then was she no more.

Aingeal had the lad christened Calogrenant Ninian, and when Calogrenant was of age, Aingeal fostered him as a page in the court of King Leodegrance of Cameliard where his half-sister was queen.

Aingeal lived alone in his castle to the end of his days, for no lady could he seek who might compare in beauty or wit with the Lady of Brocéliande. And ever thus it is with fairies and mortals, for fairy love, however strong, is but a capricious thing.

YOU'RE BACK, THEN.

AYE, MY QUEEN, AND--
SAVE YOUR BREATH, MY LADY.
I KNOW WHO YOU MET, I KNOW WHO SHE IS TO YOU, AND I KNOW WHAT YOU AND I ARE TO EACH OTHER.
AND I KNOW THAT YOUR POWERS ARE GREATER THAN MINE.

AND I KNOW THAT I LOVE TAKING THE GINGER OUT OF YOU.

Breaking fast with gossip of the court...
WORD HATH REACHED US THAT OUR COUSIN THE QUEEN HATH A PARAMOUR...
'TIS TRUE, I FEAR.

AND LANCELOT, NO LESS!
OH! SAY NOT SO!

IMAGINE TAKING THAT HULKING GAULISH GIT AS A LOVER!

YE BE RIGHT BLISSFUL THIS MORN, M'LADIES.

A PENNY FER YER THOUGHTS...

I HAVE SOME PLOTTING TO DO...
I MUST PRACTICE MY TELEPORTATION.
MY LION NEEDETH FEEDING.
ZIP
FOOM
ZIP

WELL, LADY NINIANNE, I FEAR THERE IS NOTHING MORE I CAN TEACH YOU.
AYE, MY QUEEN, AND THOU HAST TAUGHT ME WELL. UPON THE MORROW, I SHALL RETURN TO LORD MYRDDYN.

AS I SAID THIS MORNING, I AM IMPRESSED. YOU HAVE GREAT PROWESS AND ACUITY... AND I THANK YOU FOR YOUR KINDNESS TO YVAINNE...

OH, DAMN AND BLAST! I AM GOING TO MISS YOU!
WE SUFFER TOGETHER THEN, MY QUEEN FOR I FEAR I FEEL THE SAME.

I HATE YOU.
I KNOW, MY QUEEN, AND I HATE YOU, TOO.

WILL YOU TRANSPORT BACK TO CAMELOT?
NAY, MY QUEEN. I RIDE UPON THE MORROW.

I SHALL SEE YOU IN THE MORNING, THEN.
MY LADY!

TALIESIN!

I HAVE BUSINESS AT COURT AND MUST RIDE UPON THE MORROW AS WELL. I SHOULD BE HONORED BY THY COMPANY.

THE FINEST BARD IN BRITAIN IS HONORED TO RIDE WITH ME?
MY LADY, THOU ART TOO MODEST. WE LEAVE AT THY PLEASURE. UNTIL THEN I BID THEE GOOD NIGHT.

...I have been an eagle,
I have been a coracle in the sea,
I have been complaint in the banquet,
I have been a drop in a shower;
I have been a sword in the grasp of a hand,
I have been a shield in battle,
I have been a string in a harp,
disguised for nine years...*
GOOD RIDDANCE. THERE IS ONLY SO MUCH OF EITHER OF THEM I CAN TAKE.
OH, MOTHER!
* From "Cad Goddeu" or "The Battle of the Trees" Translation by Rev. Robert Williams
'TIS SAID THERE IS A MAIDEN'S BROKEN HEART FOR EACH OF TALIESIN'S HARP STRINGS.
I'VE HEARD THAT AS WELL. I AM SURE THRE IS ROOM FOR ONE MORE.
Here endeth Book II

Explicationibus sint instructae et insedit notulas (Explanatory notes and miscellaneous what-nots...)

Page 1 – 14 The Horned Man , the consort of the Green Lady of Broceliande, has many incarnations with many names, ranging through the histories and mythologies of Europe and beyond. One prominent embodiment is Cernunnos, the Celtic god of fertility, life, animals, wealth, and the underworld. In England, Herne the Hunter is said to haunt Windsor Forest and Windsor Great Park, with sightings as late as the 1920's. Shakespeare's description of him as a ghost in *The Merry Wives of Windsor* hearkens back to the Pagan deity.

Sometime a keeper here in Windsor Forest,
Doth all the winter-time, at still midnight,
Walk round about an oak, with great ragg'd horns;
And there he blasts the tree, and takes the cattle,
And makes milch-kine yield blood, and shakes a chain
In a most hideous and dreadful manner.
You have heard of such a spirit, and well you know
The superstitious idle-headed eld
Receiv'd, and did deliver to our age,
This tale of Herne the Hunter for a truth.

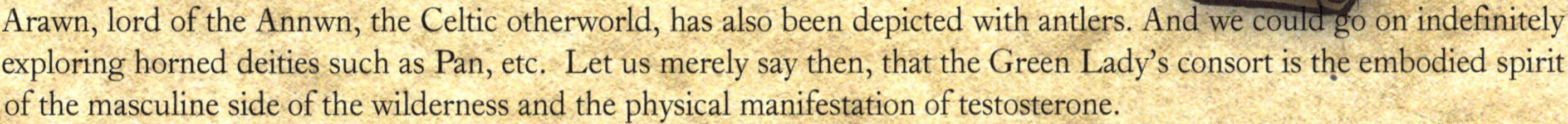

Arawn, lord of the Annwn, the Celtic otherworld, has also been depicted with antlers. And we could go on indefinitely exploring horned deities such as Pan, etc. Let us merely say then, that the Green Lady's consort is the embodied spirit of the masculine side of the wilderness and the physical manifestation of testosterone.

Page 8 – 9 Spectral Hounds have a special place in the lore of Britain. The Welsh have the Cwn Annwn, and the Cornish tell of the *Devil's Dandy Dogs. The Gabriel Ratchets* in Lancashire have human heads (the prospect of experiencing would keep me in the pub for several subsequent pints of the local bitter). Most are connected with the Wild Hunt, which we'll see later. And, of course, we must not forget that this tradition was the source of *The Hound of the Baskervilles.* Take 'ee no fear, though; they all be illusion. P'raps.

Page 10 Snails... Knights fighting snails permeate the marginalia of medieval manuscripts, but though many scholars have posited reasons, nobody has yet come up with a definitive reason. There is snail and slug imagery in Asian art and in the religious art of Meso-America. And it cannot be denied that the wetter the climate, the bigger the mollusks get. It has been posited that the Loch Ness Monster is a giant slug (which is as plausible a theory as any, I suppose), and in Marion Zimmer Bradley's *The Mists of Avalon,* Lancelot and Pellinore battle a very mollusk-like dragon. (For the record, mollusks creep me out, and my skin was crawling with every line of this page.)

Orkney
Picts
Angles, Saxons,
Jutes, Frisians, etc.
Lothian
Gorre
Hibernia
Cameliard
Myrddyn's
Cottage
Broceliande
[Because it bloody
well feels like it]
Camelot
Britain
and Environs
as located in this Tale
Brocéliande
[Supposedly]

Page 11 – 12 The Wild Hunt can be seen in folklore throughout Western Europe. The Horned Man and spectral hounds are very often, but not always, associated with it. In Germanic areas, the Hunt is led by Odin, in parts of Wales, the leader is Gwynn ap Nudd, who is sometimes mortal and sometimes king of the Fair Folk and synonymous with the Horned Man. The Hunt can be a warning of disaster, but often it is also a hunt for human bodies and souls to take off to Faerie.

It seems obvious that W.B. Yeats is describing one manifestation of the Hunt in his poem, "The Hosting of the Sidhe."

The host is riding from Knocknarea
And over the grave of Clooth-na-Bare;
Caoilte tossing his burning hair,
And Niamh calling Away, come away:
Empty your heart of its mortal dream.
The winds awaken, the leaves whirl round,
Our cheeks are pale, our hair is unbound,
Our breasts are heaving, our eyes are agleam,
Our arms are waving, our lips are apart;
And if any gaze on our rushing band,
We come between him and the deed of his hand,
We come between him and the hope of his heart.
The host is rushing 'twixt night and day,
And where is there hope or deed as fair?
Caoilte tossing his burning hair,
And Niamh calling Away, come away.

Wodens Wilde Jagd F.W. Heine

Page 13 – 14 Cally makes an offering of fruit and ale to the Horned Man. I am not making a religious statement here. The Horned Man has manifested himself to her before, and she has had direct contact with the Green Lady. Throughout the world we will find syncretisms, the blending of belief systems. In Celtic countries, particularly in Ireland, devout Christians still respect and propitiate the "Good People," and many honestly claim personal experiences. Cally has not lost her Christianity, but the borders of her faith are being widened, which is, as far as I am concerned, a good thing.

Page 15 Saxons, Picts, Kerns, Gallowglasses… If I had to give this story a time period, I would give it the same perameters as T.H. White gives for Uther Pendragon's lifetime in the *Sword in the Stone*: 1066-1216, though I must admit that much is either far earlier or far later. In *Book the First*, I was well aware of the irony of Myrddyn requesting that Cally speak in "plain English," a language which did not exist at all during Myrddyn's and Arthur's lifetimes – if they existed at all. The Saxons of this book are not the Saxons of history. They are an outside threat to Arthur's security, and that is it. Picts, a Celtic people in what is today Scotland, would also have posed a threat, but by the time of the Norman Conquest and the composing of the Arthurian romances, they would have been subsumed by the Gaelic-speaking Irish Scoti and the Norse. A kern or ceithernach was an Irish light-infantryman and part of a company of Gallóglaigh or Gallowglasses, axe-wielding mercenaries. Again, there is a time-glitch here, as these bands of warriors were in operation between the 13th and 16th centuries. But if Shakespeare can have them forming MacDonwald's rebel army in *Macbeth* sometime in the 1050's, then I can use them as well.

Page 16 – 17 Uriens (or Urien, 490 - 586 CE) was the historical king of Rheged, which, in this narrative, is identified as Gorre. He was a fierce opponent of the invading Anglo-Saxons and was instrumental in unifying the North until he was ultimately assassinated at the behest of another Northern lord. The romances have wed Uriens to Morgan Le Fay, and all the rest is legend.

Page 18 Morgan Le Fay has always been a fascinating figure for me. She is often cast as a double-dyed villainess who is carrying out a blood feud against Arthur for the murder of her father, and yet in romances like Robert de Bicket's "The Lay of the Horn" and the anonymous "Sir Gawain and the Green Knight," it is she who tests the moral fiber of Arthur's knights and does her best to warn him about the illicit affair between Lancelot and Guenevere. And what are we to make of the fact that she is one of the queens on the barge that bears the wounded Arthur to Avalon to be healed of his wounds? I never thought she was evil. Machiavellian and cynical, perhaps, but not evil. I've taken some liberties in her backstory, but I certainly wouldn't be the first to put a particular spin on her or other Arthurian characters.

I've depicted Morgan with a raven partly because she is often equated with the Irish Morrígan, a goddess of fate and battle who often takes the form of a raven or crow (though despite the dark similarities, the names are linguistically different), and the fact that there are three ravens on the arms of Rheged. (Which were not contemporary to the historical Arthurian time.) And I like ravens.

Page 23 Morgan's chamber is not unlike the living rooms of many of my friends. Her objets d'arte are:

1. Sekhmet: The Egyptian goddess of the sun, war, destruction, plagues and healing. She is a daughter of Ra and protects the Pharaoh in time of war. Though she is a healing goddess, she also wreaks havoc on those who would upset disobey the precepts of Ma'at (order and harmony) and bring disorder.
2. Hecate: The classical goddess of magic, necromancy, and the moon, She is a seer into the future and into the world of the dead, despite the darkness of her personality, she is the protectress of women and of the poor.
3. Kali: The fierce Hindu destroyer of evil and of the ego. She is a queller of demons but also brings about Moksha or enlightenment.
4. Ishtar, Inanna, Astarte, Lilith (and many other names): is the Mesopotamian goddess of love, motherhood, power, and war. She is loving and nurturing but dangerous and capricious when disobeyed.
5. Pallas Athena: The virgin Greek goddess of wisdom and warfare. Her pallid bust is placed over the chamber door, perfect for ravens to perch upon.
6. Brigid: The Celtic goddess of the hearth the forge, poetry, healing, childbirth, unity, and wells. A coin tossed into a wishing well is the survival of offerings to her.
7. The Labyrinth: The visual manifestation of the journey into the Great Mother and back out. It is not a maze as there are no wrong turns.

Page 30 Honor Killing: I have deliberately left the nationality and religion of this brother and sister ambiguous. The fact is that honor killing is not limited to Muslims, as we are currently led to believe. It is not about belief at all, but about patriarchy and the idea that a woman is property rather than her own person. The woman also alludes to the fact that she has suffered female circumcision, another practice that has little to do with faith and everything to do with the subjugation of women.

Page 31 Two Spirit and Hijra: Indigenous American tribes, as well as other tribal people throughout the world, respected and revered transgender people, who were seen to have been touched by the spirit world. Such individuals were valued for their spiritual power and insight. In more settled cultures, such as Anatolia and India, trans people were part of priesthoods and sisterhoods. This survives today in the Hijra of India, though respect for them, as with the North American "Two Spirits." was nearly destroyed by patriarchal colonists. Their status has grown again in recent years.

Page 36 Tintagel: It is certain that there was a castle at Tintagel on the northern coast of Cornwall, and it is equally certain that it didn't look like this. When I visited the ruins in the late 70's and early 80's, they were identified as 12th century. This August (2016), archeologists finished a 5-year dig with the conclusion that there was also something going on here in the much earlier, in the 5th and 6th centuries. The foundations of walls and the presence of Mediterranean pottery shards strongly suggest that someone was eating well in a well-fortified building during the prime Arthurian period. The press hailed it as a dark age palace, but the archeologists are a bit more guarded. My image is certainly based upon the geography of Tintagel, but the castle (like most of my castles) is an amalgam of several medieval fortresses.

I have to admit to taking certain liberties with the characters of the duke of Cornwall, his wife, and younger daughter. Actually there are very few clues in the romances as to exactly how Gorlois, Igerne, and their children all felt about one another. I would assume, however, that the standard medieval attitude toward wives and daughters at any level of society would be that they were property to be used in political bargaining. I recently saw an Internet meme which read, "I want to be treated like a princess." "Fine, I will marry you to the king of Poland as part of the treaty." Hence Gorlois' impatience at his daughters' temporal obstinacy and Morgause's marriage to King Lot of Lothian and Orkney. From this union shall spring four of Arthur's knights, Gawain, Agravain, Gaheris, and Gareth, and later, through either trickery or a gross inattention to detail, Mordred. Once more, I include Arthur's family tree.

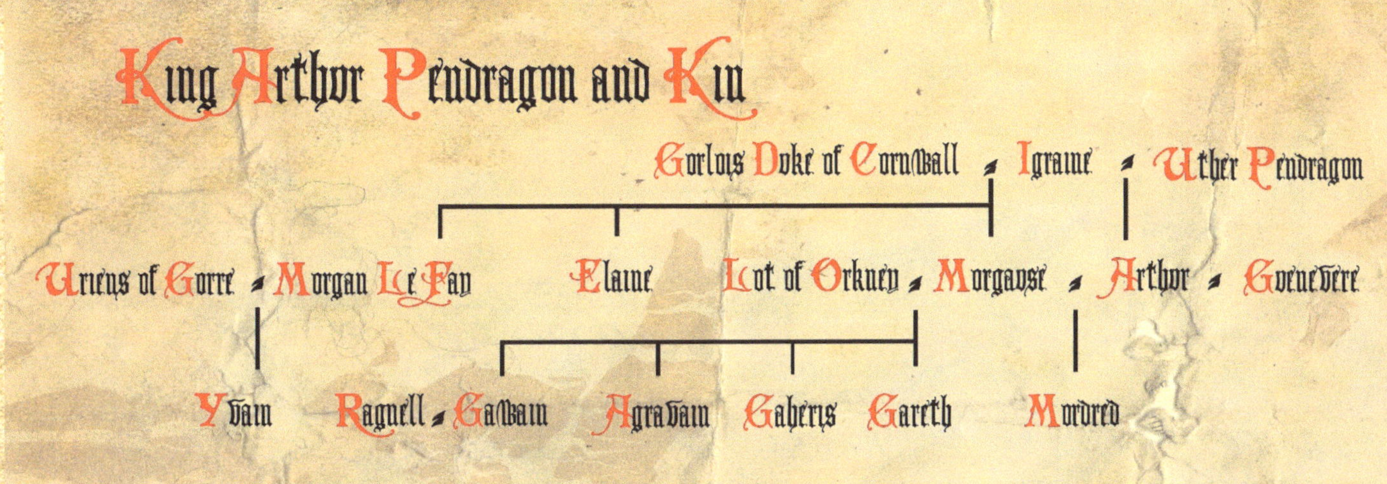

Page 39 – 52 The Birth of Arthur The story of Uther Pendragon's dalliance with a Igerne while Gorlois is out getting himself killed was first put to parchment in 1138 by Geoffrey of Monmouth in his *Historia Regium Britanniae* (History of British Kings), which marks Arthur's shift from dark-age warlord to medieval king. Most likely what Geoffrey did was to append the story of the birth of Hercules, in which Zeus disguises him self as king Amphitrion of Thebes and makes love to queen Alcmene. Again, for decades, I puzzled over Lady Igerne's obtuseness. How could she not know? I offer here a modest conjecture.

Page 48 Getting further into the true nature of Morgan's parentage, I found myself asking the question that I had asked since my teens: "Why is she called Morgan Le Fay? Morgan the fairy?" I figured this was as good a place as any to conjecture and wax mythological. While based upon real Celtic fairy lore, Morgan's Faerie pedigree derives solely from my mother wit. Arawn is one of several names of the king of the Celtic otherworld and is often conflated with the Horned Man (and is sometimes portrayed with antlers). He is a major character in the story of Pwyll in the marvelous collection of Welsh tales called *The Mabionogion.*

Page 49 – 50 The Ballad of Amalud and the Green Lady is of my own composition, but it incorporates elements of many tales of liaisons between mortals and fairies.

Page 52 N.C.W. The initials behind Morgan stand for N.C. Wyeth (1882 – 1945), one of the finest American illustrators ever, and whose images helped to solidify the Arthurian legend visually for generations. I couldn't hope to replicate his mastery, but I could, at least steal his composition.

Page 56 – Caillich in Scots Gaelic means "Hag," and though one wonders about giving an infant that name, it suits Misstress Caillic perfectly. The name is directly related to The Cailleach of Scotland, Ireland, and the Isle of Man. She is the Crone, "She Who Knows," and is the embodiment of winter. The fact that her cat is named Graymalkin might give a hint regarding other aspects of her life.

Page 59 – Cuchulain, the teenage warrior who single-handedly defended Ulster from an invasion by the Army of Maeve of Connacht, while the Red Branch Warriors were laid low with the pangs of birth (the tale of which I shall not relate here) was famous for his Warp of Battle or Warp Spasm that came upon him when his Irish was up.

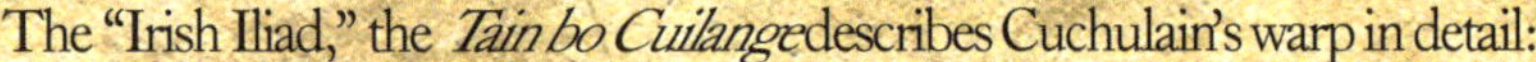

The "Irish Iliad," the *Tain bo Cuilange* describes Cuchulain's warp in detail:

> *Then took place the first twisting-fit and rage of the royal hero Cuchulain, so that he made a terrible, many-shaped, wonderful, unheard of thing of himself. His flesh trembled about him like a pole against the torrent or like a bulrush against the stream, every member and every joint and every point and every knuckle of him from crown to ground. He made a mad whirling-feat of his body within his hide. His feet and his shins and his knees slid so that they came behind him. His heels and his calves and his hams shifted so that they passed to the front. The muscles of his calves moved so that they came to the front of his shins, so that each huge knot was the size of a soldier's balled fist. He stretched the sinews of his head so that they stood out on the nape of his neck, hill-like lumps, huge, incalculable, vast, immeasurable and as large as the head of a month-old child.*
>
> *He next made a ruddy bowl of his face and his countenance. He gulped down one eye into his head so that it would be hard work if a wild crane succeeded in drawing it out on to the middle of his cheek from the rear of his skull. Its mate sprang forth till it came out on his cheek. His mouth was distorted monstrously. He drew the cheek from the jaw-bone so that the interior of his throat was to be seen. His lungs and his lights stood out so that they fluttered in his mouth and his gullet. He struck a mad lion's blow with the upper jaw on its fellow so that as large as a wether's fleece of a three year old was each red, fiery flake which his teeth forced into his mouth from his gullet.*
>
> *There was heard the loud clap of his heart against his breast like the yelp of a howling bloodhound or like a lion going among bears. There were seen the torches of the Badb, and the rain clouds of poison, and the sparks of glowing-red fire, blazing and flashing in hazes and mists over his head with the seething of the truly wild wrath that rose up above him. His hair bristled all over his head like branches of a redthorn thrust into a gap in a great hedge. Had a king's apple-tree laden with royal fruit been shaken around him, scarce an apple of them all would have passed over him to the ground, but rather would an apple have stayed stuck on each single hair there, for the twisting of the anger which met it as it rose from his hair above him.*
>
> *The Lon Laith ('Champion's Light') stood out of his forehead, so that it was as long and as thick as a warrior's whetstone. As high, as thick, as strong, as steady, as long as the sail-tree of some huge prime ship was the straight spout of dark blood which arose right on high from the very ridge-pole of his crown, so that a black fog of witchery was made thereof like to the smoke from a king's hostel what time the king comes to be ministered to at nightfall of a winter's day.*

Tr. Joseph Dunn (1914)

Page 60 The *Awen* can be translated as "inspiration." Its Irish equivalent, "*Imbas Forosnai*," is "Fire in the Head." Considering the power invested in poets by the Celts (a bard is one step below a Druid) this fire of inspiration can be considered a connection with the cosmos and the creative energy that lies within all of us. But there are some who have a naturally stronger relationship to this energy. In most Shamanic traditions, one does not realize one's self as a shaman because it is an ambition; one is a shaman because one is a shaman.

Page 65 The shard of clay tablet reads, "IF YOU CAN READ THIS YOU CAN BECOME A SCRIBE AND GET A GOOD JOB," in Babylonian cuneiform. The fact that something is ancient does not mean it cannot be mundane. Life is life.

Page 72 Sir Gawain's belt – In the anonymous 14th century romance, "Sir Gawain and the Green Knight," Gawain accepts a challenge from an enchanted green knight to exchange blows. Gawain beheads the knight, who nonchalantly picks up his head and tells Gawain to meet him a year hence to receive the same treatment. After politely refusing the sexual advances of the lady of a castle near the appointed Green Chapel, Gawain finally accepts a green belt, or girdle, from her, which she says will render him invulnerable. The Green Knight, who turns out to be the lady's husband, spares Gawain's life because he had passed a test of honor and chastity (set up, unsurprisingly by Morgan Le Fay), but he gives Gawain a nick from his axe for having accepted the belt – which anyone would have done. Chagrined, Gawain wears the girdle from then on. The romancer tells us that the belt is emblazoned with the motto: "HONI SOIT QUI MAL Y PENSE," or "Shame be to him who thinks evil of it," (which I've always interpreted as, "To hell with you if you can't take a joke.") It is the motto of the Order of the Garter to this day.

Page 76 – 88 Yvain, like Uriens, was a real person, known to the chroniclers as Ewan or Owain. As mentioned on page 88, there is an intriguing possibility regarding Yvain's gender. In a fragmentary 12th century *Life of St. Kentigern*, Prince Owan ab Urien impregnates Teneu, the daughter of King Leudonis, who was to become King Lot, father of Gawain and his brothers, in the Arthurian romances. According to the saint's life, Teneu wanted to emulate the Virgin Mary, and Owain came to her dressed as a woman, convincing her that she would not lose her virginity by sleeping with a woman. The result is that Teneu became pregnant with the child who would later become St. Kentigern, otherwise known as St. Mungo, Apostle to Strathclyde and patron saint of the City of Glasgow. The story is both farcical and cruel and reflects horribly upon Yvain/Owain. However, in his book *Finding Merlin: The Truth Behind the Legend of the Great Arthurian Mage,* historian Adam Ardrey argues that since Teneu was not kept in a convent or a seraglio, there was no need for Owain to present as female other than identity. As I suggest in the text, I find this argument rather tenuous, but it does give me a chance to look at another aspect of being transgender.

Pages 88 – 90 The Goddess. Through my years of coming to consciousness as a transgender woman, I found the mainstay of my support within the Goddess community. Ironically, about the time I was drawing this sequence, I found myself at odds with a transphobic group within that community. From the first, my questions about being trans were overwhelmingly spiritual. As I researched, I discovered a surprising amount of information about the history of trans spirituality and its connection (and, at times, inseparability) from women's spirituality in general. The images herein come from that vast history. Cally. Morgan, and Caillic represent, of course, the three aspects of the Divine Feminine, but I think the iconography on page 82 deserves some commentary.

1. The Labyrinth: Again we see the visual representation of the journey into the Great Mother and back out, variations of which appear beneath the palace of Knossis on Crete, in the ridges of Glastonbury Tor, and on the floor of the nave of Chartres Cathedral, amongst many other places.
2. Isis: Sister and consort of Osiris and mother of Horus the younger. A goddess of life, nurturing, and compassion.
3. Pomegranates: A symbol of the goddesses Hera, containing the seeds of life and representing life and death, rebirth and eternal life, fertility and marriage, and abundance.
4. Bees have been connected with the sacred and particularly with the Mother Goddess throughout history and (at least) throughout the West.

5. Hecate: this page is rife with triplets, and this particular triplet is the graphic representation of Hecate.
6. The Cow is, more than almost any beast, a representation of The Mother. In Egypt, the goddesses Isis and Hathor are seen with bovine heads, and in Norse lore, it was the cow Audhumla who licked away the ice block that imprisoned Ymir and then fed this progenitor of gods, giants, and humans with her milk.
7. Sekhmet, and Bast are the Egyptian feline manifestations of the mother.
8. Demeter/Ceres, the classical goddess of the fields is represented by the sheaf of wheat.
9. Poppies are also symbolic of Demeter and of death and resurrection.

Page 89 -91 Cally's begetting is inspired, as is Morgan's, by several tales of liaisons of fairies and mortals, but particularly by the story of Melulsine, first told in full by Jean d'Arras in 1387. Sabine Baring-Gould retells the story beautifully in his book *Curious Myths of the Middle Ages*, but his version is too lengthy to print here, but Funk and Wagnall's Standard Dictionary of Folklore Mythology and Legend gives a concise version. (If you can find a copy of Baring-Gould's book, snap it up. It's delightful!)

> *Elinus, king of Scotland, married the fairy Pressina. To this marriage was attached the lying-in tabu: the husband might not see the wife in the lying-in chamber. After three daughters were born, Melusine, Melior, and Plantina, Elinus broke the tabu, and Pressina returned to Avalon. Melusine, when she grew older, imprisoned her father in a mountain, for which act, her mother ordered that she become a serpent from the waist down every Saturday. Yet, if she could find a husband who would agree not to see her on Saturdays, she might obtain release from this punishment and die naturally. She was discovered by Count Raymond of Lusignan bathing in a woodland spring. They married; he agreed to observe the tabu. But her many sons were born each with some defect. One of Raymond's brothers convinced him finally that Melusine's Saturday retreats were made in order to entertain a lover. (Monstrous children are commonly believed to be the offspring of illegitimate love.) Raymond broke into her room and saw her, half-serpent, bathing. Nothing was said then, but later, during quarrel, a he called her a "false serpent." She left at once, and he never saw her again. As she fled, she left a footprint outside a window of the castle: a corroborating bit of evidence for tellers of the local legend. Melusine returned to nurse her children and could be heard flying around the castle, crying mournfully.*

There are also elements borrowed from the Hindu story of Prince Sudyamna from the *Srimad-Bhagavatam*, in which a boy child was meant to be a girl and was eventually restored to that gender.

Page 97 – Taliesin is another Arthurian figure who may have been an actual historical personage – a bard to which many poems are attributed. Information about him is scanty, though, and his figure is shadowy. And so it shall remain until *Book the Third.*

A Selective Bibliography

(Which is the author's way of saying that these are the books which she has used in research, alluded to or quoted in one way or another, was influenced by, or has laying around the house...)

ARTHURIAN, MYTHIC, AND SPIRITUAL...

Alcock, Leslie. *Arthur's Britain.* Hammondsworth: Penguin, 1971.

--------. *Was this Camelot? Excavations at Cadbury Castle 1966-70.* New York: Stein and Day, 1972.

Ardrey, Adam. F*inding Merlin: the Truth behind the Legend of the Great Arthurian Mage.* Woodstock and New York: Overlook Press, 2008.

Ashe, Geoffrey. *Camelot and the Vision of Albion.* Saint Albans: Granada, 1971.

--------. editor. *The Quest for Arthur's Britain.* Saint Albans: Granada, 1971.

--------. *The Discovery of King Arthur.* New York: Doubleday, 1985.

--------. *King Arthur's Avalon: The Ttory of Glastonbury.* Glasgow: Collins, 1957.

Ashley, Mike. *The Mammoth Book of King Arthur.* London: Robinson, 2005.

Bloom, Harold, ed. Bloom's *Major Literary Characters: King Arthur.* Philadelphia: Chelsea House, 2004.

Bradley, Marion Zimmer. *The Mists of Avalon.* New York: Alfred Knopf, 1982.

Brengle, Richard L. ED. *Arthur King of Britain: History, Chronicle, Romance, and Criticism.* Englewood Cliffs, New Jersey: Prentice Hall, 1964.

Burger, Thomas. *Arthur Rex: A Legendary Novel.* New York Delta, 1978.

Chaucer, Geoffrey. *The Wyf of Bathe.* Illustrated by Gregory Irons. San Francisco: Bellerophon Books, 1973.

Chretien de Troyes. *Perceval or the Story of the Grail.* Ruth Harwood Cline, translator. Athens, Georgia: University of Georgia press, 1983.

--------. Yvan: The Knight of the Lion. Burton Ruffel, translator. New haven: Yale UP, 1987.

Cowan, Tom. *Fire in the Head: Shamanism and Celtic Spirit.* San Francisco: Harper, 1993.

Cummins, W. A. *King Arthur's Place in Prehistory: The Great Age of Stonehenge.* Godalming, Surrey: Bramley Book,1992.

Darrah, John. *The Real Camelot: Paganism and the Arthurian Romances.* London: Thames and Hudson, 1981.

Geoffrey of Monmouth. History of the Kings of Britain. Sebastien Evans translator. New York: Dutton, 1958.

Hall, Louis B. *The Knightly Tales of Sir Gawain.* Chicago: Nelson-Hall, 1976.

Hastings, Selina. *Sir Gawain and the Loathly Lady.* Illustrated by Juan Wijgaard. New York: Morrow, 1987.

Jung, Emma and Marie-Louise von Franz. *The Grail Legend.* Boston: Sigo press, 1980.

Lacey, Noris Jay, Ed. *The Arthurian Encyclopedia.* New York: Peter Bedrick, 1987.

Loomis, Roger Sherman, ed. *Arthurian Literature in the Middle Ages: A Collaborative History.* Oxford UP, 1959.

Mabonogion. Jeffrey Ganz, translator. Hammondsworth: Penguin, 1976.

Malory, Sir Thomas. Le Morte d'Arthur. New York: Modern Library, 1999.

Matthews, John. *King Arthur: Dark Age Warrior and Mythic Hero.* New York: Random House, 2004.

--------, ed. *Sources of the Grail: An Anthology.* Hudson, New York: Lindisfarne Press, 1997.

--------. *King Arthur and the Grail Quest, Myth and Vision from Celtic Times to the Present.* London: Brockhampton Press, 1995.

--------. *The Book of Arthur: Lost Tales from the Round Table.* Old Saybrook, Connecticut: Konecky , 2002.

--------. *The Song of Taliesin: Tales from King Arthur's Bard.* Wheaton, IL:Quest Books, 2001

Matthews, Caitlyn and John. *King Arthur's Raid on the Underworld: The Oldest Grail Quest.* Paintings by Meg Falconer. Glastonbury: Gothic Image, 2008.

Morris, John. *The Age of Arthur: A History of the British Isles from 350 to 650.* New York: Scribners, 1973.

Monaco, Richard. *Parsival or a Knight's Tale.* New York: McMillan, 1977.

--------. *The Grail War.* New York: Simon and Schuster, 1979.

--------. *The Final Quest.* New York: Putnam, 1981.

Nye, Robert. *Merlin.* London: Hamish Hamilton, 1978

Stewart, Mary. *The Crystal Cave.* London: Hodder & Stoughton, 1970.

--------. *The Hollow Hills.* London: Hodder & Stoughton, 1973.

--------. *The Last Enchantment.* London: Hodder & Stoughton, 1979.

--------. *The Wicked Day.* London: Hodder & Stoughton, 1983.

Suttcliff, Rosemary. *The Sword at Sunset.* London: Hodder & Stoughton, 1963.

Tennyson, Alfred. Idylls of the King. New York: New American Library, 1961.

The Quest of the Holy Grail. P. M. Matarasso translator. Hammondsworth: Penguin, 1969.

Tolstoy, Nikolai. The Quest for Merlin. Boston: Little Brown, 1985.

Trlyndru, Jhenah. *Avalon Within: A Sacred Journey of Myth, Mystery, and Inner Wisdom.* Woodbury, Minnesota: Llewellyn. 2005.

Wace and Layamon. *Arthurian Chronicles* Eugene Mason tr. New York: Dutton, Everyman's Library. 1912. Reprinted 1972.

Weston, Jesse L. *From Ritual to Romance.* Cambridge UP, 1920

White, T. H. *The Book of Merlyn.* Austin Texas: University of Texas press, 1977.

--------. *The Once and Future King.* New York: Putnam, 1958.

--------. The Sword in the Stone. London: Collins, 1938

(White revised *The Sword in the Stone* for inclusion in *The Once and Future King* and incoporated *The Book of Merlyn* into both that and the "Candle in the Wind" chapter of the book.)

Wolfram Von Eschenbach,. *Parzival.* Helen M. Mustard and Charles E. Passage, translators. New York: Random, 1961.

Specific to Gender...

There are many books on gender and transgender issues at present. After lifetimes of being relegated to the sensational, the subject is finally getting wide attention. These books, however, should make up the core reading of anyone who is coming to terms with being transgender or is trying to understand someone who is. They are both readable and humanizing. I include *The Chalice and the Blade* here not because it is specifically about transgenderism (it is not), but because it acknowledges the spiritual position of trans women in pre-patriarchal societies.

Bornstein, Kate. *Gender Outlaw: On Men, Women, and the Rest of Us.* New York. Psychology Press, 1994.

Boylan, Jennifer Finney. *She's Not There: A Life in Two Genders.* New York: Random, 2003.

Eisler, Riane *The Chalice and the Blade: Our History, Our Future.* San Francisco: Harper, 1987.

Erickson-Schroth, Laura. *Trans Bodies, Trans Selves: A Resource for the Transgender Community.* Oxford UP, 2014

Feinberg, Leslie. *Transgender Warriors: Making History from Joan of Arc to Dennis Rodman.* Boston: Beacon, 1997.

Mock, Janet. *Redefining Realness: My Path to Womanhood, Identity, Love & So Much More.* New York: Simon & Schuster, 2014.

About Gillian...

illian Cameron has been blessed with two among many attributes: a lifelong fascination with folklore and mythology and a gender identity which goes beyond the traditional masculine and feminine roles. Through two decade of storytelling and three of teaching in both secondary and college classrooms, she has found that perhaps the most significant insights into the transgender experience are contained within the collective unconscious – within the stories passed down as part of the oral and written heritage of cultures worldwide.

Throughout her careers as educator, writer and storyteller, Gillian has collected stories from such varied cultures and periods as ancient Greece, India, Russia, Scotland and the Americas, which explore the mythic and mystical side of what it means to be human.

Of course, at the center of this fascination with the archetypal is a life-long love of the Arthurian legend, which manifested early in Gillian's childhood, when The Adventures of Sir Lancelot came on right after The Mickey Mouse Club.

Another great love in Gillian's life is comic art. By her own admission, Gillian worships the ground trod upon by cartoonists and animators and particularly admires the work of Walt Kelly, René Goscinny and Albert Uderzo, Chuck Jones, Gregory Irons, and Jack Davis, to name a few. Calogrenant has been a challenge and a learning experience for her, and has loved every second of the project.

As she enters her crone years, Gillian looks forward to exploring more with Calogrenant and other projects, raising awareness, asking questions, discovering more of her authenticity, and always hoping to make people smile.